The

Foreign

Exchange

SEAN SCOTT KERNS

Library of Congress Number 1917639

ISBN: 099105461X
ISBN-13:978-0991054619

DEDICATION

For my Uncle Billy,

the blueprint of

a good and peaceful man.

CONTENTS

ACKNOWLEDGMENTS

A special thanks to mi familia for their love and support. Another big thanks to my trip advisor Angela, my editor and translator FI, and keeping-it-real proofreader and mentor Clarissa.

Prologue

Nine men sat at the oval table with the rector or chairman at the head. He said, "Now that the annual faculty gala matter is concluded, the last item on our agenda is the professor for the foreign exchange program. They have been interviewed by a panel of composed leadership and these are the recommendations. This year our top three candidates are from America. The candidates are as follows: Dr. Maxwell Privot; Kentucky Commonwealth University in Kentucky, Dr. Katherine Lutz; Lemands University in Texas; and Dr. Mychal Ayscue; Queens City University in

New York."

"Says here that Privot is in education, Lutz is in journalism fundamentals and Ayscue is in English." The old man to the chairman's left looked over the sheet again, then said to the chairman, "I vote out the woman."

"Joseph, you are not being fair," the chairman replied.

The chancellor interrupted them by saying, "What about Dr. Ayscue? He has his doctorate from a well-known university, was a committee member on a number of dissertations and university research projects, and wrote a book in his field about how support for freshman reading labs could factor into retention and graduation rates. Actually, his field is more of what we are looking for. Also, we could use his research knowledge to improve the university's reading and writing labs both on campus and online."

"I see what you mean. I too was impressed by the book. I think we should look no further. He's our man," said the chairman. The group voiced their agreement. "I need a motion."

Chancellor Lomas made the recommendation to hire Dr. Ayscue for the foreign exchange position and immediately got a second motion. The motion was carried with no opposition. "It's agreed then. Guillermo, make sure your secretary sends him the letter as well as informing the others that the position was filled but we will keep their applications on file. I make a motion that this meeting be adjourned."

A second motion came immediately.

"Good day gentlemen." The meeting was over, but some board members lingered in separate conversations.

The chairman was just about to close the folder when he noticed a blank on the application. *Christo*, he thought, by the time things got to the board they were supposed to be double checked. Then again, Guillermo's secretary was new, replacing the previous one who was old and grouchy, but detail oriented. Picking up his pen, the chairman went to the unmarked box on the applicant sheet marked gender and checked male beside the chosen candidate.

1
Decisions and Dysfunction

It had to be the hardest day of Mychal Ayscue's life. She stood at the security checkpoint leading to her terminal surrounded by her family members, with the exception of her sister. Quietly, she gave her older brother last minute instructions, then squeezed his hand before going through security. The walk to her terminal was like a trip to a cell. While awaiting the plane's departure, Mychal took in the distant blur of the city's skyline one last time. Saying goodbye to her family and moving to Spain was a tough decision. In the long run it would be for the best. She would leave the States and return in a few years after living abroad.

Her weeks leading up to leaving were less than ideal. She could not be elated about her new position abroad due to her sister and brother-in-law. Months ago she pulled out of a business arrangement with her sister's husband, Jake. She had serious concerns about the nature of his non profit organization. Jake ran the company and Mychal was his silent partner slash silent investor. In the time Mychal worked with him, not once did she see the company donating money or goods to anything. What she did see was the profits from investments Jake made on the company's behalf. She knew how much she invested but wondered where did he get the additional funds to invest. Before opening the business, Jake was a health foods grocery store manager. When Mychal asked he told her from government grants. She demanded to see the accounting books. After weeks of avoiding her, but her insisting, he finally complied.

Mychal did not need an accountant to see the tens of thousands of grants dollars invested in the stock market. She was appalled at the salary Jake was paying himself. Then she saw line items for donations with no recipient. She had seen enough. The next day she had her brother Max, draw up the resolution to dissolve the partnership. She wanted out immediately.

Her sister, Riley, was beyond upset. She accused Mychal of attempting to destroy the business her husband worked so hard to create. Mychal was beyond shocked. What terrible story was Jake feeding her sister?

When Mychal finally confronted Riley with the truth of what was really going on in the business, her sister twisted everything. She accused Mychal of trying to ruin their lives. Then she played the sibling rivalry card by insinuating that Mychal did not want Riley to be as successful as her. Mychal responded with the same old Riley's pity party. Knowing it was childish she went on the throw in that they both knew her two younger siblings were always their mother's favorites, treating her and Max different. That comment incensed Riley so much that she threw her phone at Mychal. Seeing their conversation was moving to old disturbing ground, Mychal put her sister's phone on the table and left her house.

From that point on, every family moment was tense with Mychal leaving the event shortly after her sister arrived. Mother's Day was the worst with Mychal keeping away from her sister that afternoon. If Riley came in the room, Mychal left. After dinner, her brothers begged her to stay, but she had enough of Riley and Jake.

Things had not gotten any better up to Mychal leaving. At the dinner birthday party her brothers gave her, Riley was sullen and pouty the entire time. After their brother Reese, took her outside for a talk, her attitude was better but still standoffish. Mychal was afraid her whole awkward presence would ruin the party for family, colleagues, and community acquaintances. She breathed a sigh of relief when the guests left.

As the four siblings sat around cleaning up, they reminisced over family memories. They laughed about each siblings wedding and their mother's over the top behavior at each event. Riley made the comment that if Mychal was married she would understand how difficult it could be at times, especially when it came to family. Unable or unwilling to be civil any longer, Mychal let her sister have the full onslaught of emotions, she had been dealing with over the months.

She let her sister know how tired she was of the pity party she had been invoking since middle school. Mychal told her she was tired of Riley using both her and Max's educations as some kind of personal offence

against her. She went on the tell her sister
that she married Jacob because he promised
her the classic Italian housewife dream, but
he was really a scam artis. She went on to
say that their ideal life was built on a lie
that would one day catch up with her.
Finally she thanked her sister for ruining
one of the few days she had left in the
States with the people she loved.

They heard a gasp and all eyes turned
to look at their mother in the doorway. She
burst into tears before leaving the room.
Riley and Reese went to get her while Max
stayed with Mychal. Same as always.

That was two weeks before she left.
Mychal took the next two weeks getting her
financial affairs in place. She moved money
around to accounts for her nieces and
nephews. She gave Max her power of
attorney and important documents that he
may need to handle business in her
absence. She gave Reese her car so he could
now have two cars for his family. She
packed up her house and decided what

could be shipped to Spain, not knowing her living situation beyond that she would be staying with a host family. Mychal had every intention of contacting them and setting up a video chat, but ran out of time with all that had to be done before she left the country.

She made arrangements for her mother to move into her house in Throgs Neck. Her mother pleaded with her to make things right with her sister, but Mychal had no time and no desire. She was moving out of the country and her spoiled sister's drama would have to wait.

Suddenly Mychal felt unbearably sad under the weight of the memories from all the drama before she left. Unable to control them any longer, she let the tears roll down her face. Soon after the plane took off, she cried herself to sleep.

2

Confusion and Chaos

Mychal had been in Spain only a couple
of hours and already had a headache. The
plane ride to Barajas was uneventful but
going through customs was a circus. After
that ordeal, she hailed a porter then went to
claim her luggage. With the hustle and
bustle of the airport she was glad the
majority of her clothes and belongings were
shipped over earlier. Then, with porter in
tow she went over to the main information
desk and inquired in broken Spanish about
prearranged ground transportation. The
man behind the counter pointed to a group
of individuals holding various signs with

different names. A small weathered man whose face had tan lines from shades held a tablet with her name in English and Spanish. She walked over to him and asked did he speak English in the same broken Spanish.

"*Sí Señora.* Can I help you?"

"I hope so, because I am Dr. Ayscue. Are you my transportation?"

"*¡Perdóneme, Señora!* I did not know the doctor had a wife!" he exclaimed.

"No, you do not understand; I am Dr. Mychal Ayscue," she was losing her good temperedness.

"*Pero Señora, el Señor Ricardo* said I was here to pick up a man about thirty with a northern states accent," the man said with a worried face. "*Ninguna esposa.*"

"Okay Mr. . . . "

"Pedro."

"Pedro. Right. I can understand the mix-up. It is natural because I have a man's name. But I will make a deal with you. First, I will show you my passport, so you can verify who I am. Second, you leave word at the desk here for Dr. Ayscue anyway, just in case another Mychal Ayscue comes along and I am wrong. Next, you take me to see Chancellor Lomas and if I cannot prove to him that I am without a doubt the person he hired for the exchange program, then I will take full responsibility for any consequences that befall you. *¿Comprenda?*" She flashed him a winning smile.

"I do not know *señora*. It is not the chancellor I am worried about, it is *Señor Ricardo*."

"I don't know *Señor Ricardo* but we will just have to deal with him too because there is no way I am staying at this airport any longer behind some crazy mix-up. Now let's go to your *auto*," she signaled to the porter to follow them. Once in the sleek luxury sedan, she tried to quiz Pedro about her living arrangements. All she got was that she would be living with the host family in her own suite at the villa. The only other words were Pedro muttering under his breath about *Señor Ricardo*.

The drive was a relatively moderate commute with Mychal taking in everything from the modern office buildings to the mountains in the far distance. Upon pulling into the long driveway presumably leading to her new residence, she was amazed by the fruit trees and gorgeous floral arrangements that were lining the drive and placed throughout the lawn. The yellow and red flowers were so bright that they seemed unreal. Mychal made a mental note to come out later to touch and smell them. The lawn was perfectly manicured. The grass appeared to be an unusually vibrant shade of green. If Mychal had to guess, she would give kudos to the driver based on his weathered appearance. He looked like the type that would enjoy the serenity of gardening.

"¡Qué Bella!"

He smiled shyly but confidently, "You like it? I do much of the work myself. You should see *mis jardines magnificos*. I will show you sometime if you are allowed to stay."

Smiling at her accurate intuition, she replied, "That would be nice. Pedro, if you don't mind me saying your English is as good as your Spanish."

"Gracias. El padre del Señor Ricardo made us learn different languages when we came to work for him. We are here," he pulled in front of a massive villa. "I will escort you in and someone will get your bags later, again if you are allowed to stay."

He led her into a room lined with books and paintings with four people. Mychal noted bookcases with exquisite woodwork, a desk, bar, and paintings of handsome couples on the walls. As they entered all eyes turned to her. The tallest man in the room stood and spoke, his voice amused. "Pedro *¿Qué es esto?* I sent you to the airport to pick up Dr. Ayscue and you come back with one of Tony's girlfriends."

Strained chuckles filled the room, making the youngest man in the room blush.

"*Este es el* Dr. Ayscue," Pedro answered looking down.

"I did not know he had a wife. That was not on the application," the tall man looked puzzled.

"*Señor, escúcheme* I too have doubts. But she insisted. She even showed me her passport. So I am trying to tell you . . . " the smaller man faltered.

"He is trying to tell you that I **am** the new exchange professor," Mychal tried to explain, extending her hand. No one moved to shake it, so she quickly put it down.

Ignoring her gesture, the tall handsome man with the jet black hair said, "*¡Muy bien no más! ¿Dónde está Dr. Ayscue?*"

Trying again Mychal spoke up attempting to lightened the mood, "Okay, how about let's try this again. Hello everyone, I'm Mychal Ayscue just off the plane from New York. Surprise! My masculine name has created yet another awkward and uncomfortable situation. I get it because my good man, Pedro, did not want to believe me either. I had to make him bring me here lest I would still be at the airport. Believe me, I am *the* Dr. Ayscue. I have a valid ID. I don't have a vitae on hand but I can highlight my career; author of 'The Reading Lab Retention Graduation Correlation', tenured associate professor in English at Queens City University and the most qualified candidate for the job. I did interview for the position via video chat. But maybe someone here should have done their homework. My digital footprint is on the internet."

She flashed an even white smile with a hint of pettiness, "That point aside. Ta! Da! Your new foreign exchange professor in the flesh."

"Prove it; what was your dissertation?" came his answer in the form of a question. What did her dissertation have to do with anything? This overbearing man seemed to have it out for her.

"Easy. How the use of resources allotted to freshman like reading labs in university English departments factor into retention rates and therefore significantly affect graduation rates. Do you need my thesis too or would you just like to check my New York driver's license?" She came back smugly.

"*Hermano*! Roman Ricardo, what is your problem?" The only other woman in the room spoke up. "You want Dr. Ayscue to think she is unwelcome? Please ignore his initial introduction. My brother Roman, Richard as we call him, can seem a little roguish at times. I am Susanna Garçia-Torrés. The younger *padre* is my twin brother Antonio. But he wants to be like his older brother and goes by his American name Tony. And finally my Uncle Juandelas Lomas, the chancellor."

The chancellor spoke up, "Welcome Dr. Ayscue. What a pleasure it is to finally meet you. Regardless of this initial introduction, I hope your stay will be pleasant with the host family we have arranged for you."

The chancellor shot his older nephew a warning look.-

"You lied on your application," Richard demanded.

"I did no such thing. You saw my name and assumed like the rest of the known world that I was a man. Look, I'm sorry I didn't video call you, but you didn't call me either. Did anybody here at least Google me? Are part of the job duties growing a beard and using a urinal? Why does it matter that I am a woman? I know my field, I am good at my job, and evidently, good enough to get this job." Mychal's headache threatened to return.

"Well Dr. Ayscue, you know how men can be. Directly meaning my older brother. I know you must be tired and that extra inquiry from Richard did not help anything. Let me show you to your room." Susanna led her upstairs. Once she stood up, Mychal saw this young woman, Susanna, was a petite Spanish beauty with almost waist length raven hair. Her olive complexion appeared flawless and her hazel eyes added to her natural beauty. She moved gracefully as she swept past Mychal into the foyer and headed to the bottom of a curved staircase. Her head barely reached past Mychal's chin.

After the two women left, Richard said, "Just great. Dr. Ayscue is a woman. How will the board take this?"

"About the same way you did," answered Chancellor Lomas, "but they too will recover, just as you will. As she said we did hire her because she was the most qualified and there is no beard growing required for this position. *Sí?*"

"Have a drink Richard, watch the soccer game with us or do something. You need a drink because right now After the way you acted, you need *un barbitúrico*. You cannot be upset because like she said, you did not do your homework on her. Come on Uncle Juan." Tony picked up his own drink and left the library for the family room.

Too tired from jet lag and controlling her temper fueled headache, Mychal noticed none of her surroundings as she entered her room. All she cared about was a bed for a much needed nap. When the cloud of sleep ebbed from Mychal's brain, she looked around trying to get her bearings.

She was on a huge bed in a spacious bedroom. The wooden furnishings were offset by the navy blue, peach and grey color scheme. Beyond this room there were two columns that separated what she could see was a tastefully decorated living room. Her clothes were in a pile next to the bed and an open bottle of Naproxen on the night table. Thank God her headache was gone. She jumped at the sound of a chiming phone. It did not sound like her cell phone which at the very moment was on the table beside the bed. The noise continued, making Mychal get up to investigate. On the sliver of wall space between the bathroom and living room, hung a blinking intercom making the chiming sound. Guardedly she pushed the talk button and said, "Um, hello?"

"Dr. Ayscue I am so glad you are awake. Are you all right for dinner with the family?" The same unfriendly tone from the earlier interrogation.

"I guess. . . I guess so."

"Good. I will see you about eight. Oh, by the way, you are not dining at a burger place. I trust you will dress appropriately? We will meet in the library which is the room we were in when you came in today. Please be on time." The call abruptly ended.

'Not at a burger place' Mychal mouthed back at the intercom and pushed the end button feeling that she and *Señor* Roman, Ricardo, Richard or whatever his name was, would not be best friends. The man was an egotistical, aggressive bear of a human on her first hours in the country no less!

After a refreshing shower, she stood in front of the luggage she brought on the flight. What did they consider appropriate dress for dinner? She thought, and then went to one of the garment bags in the closet. Pulling out a white halter dress, she hung it in the bathroom where she left the shower on to get the wrinkles out. Then she hunted for her white wedge heel sandals. Several minutes later Mychal looked in the mirror at the finished product. Her dark chocolate hair and cashew colored skin were a contrast to the white dress and gold necklace. The only makeup she wore was eyeliner, eye shadow to accent her amber colored eyes, and lipstick. She smiled at her image thinking 'damn right, I am the right woman for this job', then whisked out of the room.

When she went downstairs, she went to the only room she knew. Everyone seemed to be waiting for her. She flashed a dazzling smile as she entered the room and inquired, "Am I late?"

"No," answered Tony, "we, on occasion, have cocktails. What will you have? I am not a bartender, but I can mix liquors and a chaser."

She nodded negatively, indicating she would not be drinking a cocktail tonight. She needed to be on point tonight. After the afternoon's introduction, she did not know what to expect.

"Then may I say Dr. Ayscue that you look lovely this evening."

Susanna nodded in agreement, "Yes, very different from the jeans and jacket you arrived in earlier today."

Richard just frowned, although he had to admit to himself she was quite striking. He had been so shocked and upset when she arrived that he only saw her as a problem. Now she stood talking with his siblings as though they were old friends. The white material of her dress somehow looked brighter against her cashew colored skin. Her dark chocolate hair was pulled back into a loose ponytail and her makeup was so light it seemed natural as if it was her own face. Only the muted crimson lipstick she wore made her lips, curved in a smile, the most noticeable part of her face. She was indeed as his brother said, lovely.

"Thank you. Please, no more formalities since I guess I will be staying here. She shot Richard a questioning look. He did not reply. "Dr. Ayscue sounds so old and collegial. Please, please, call me Mychal."

"Good, now that you have made that clear, we can eat." Richard spoke and left the room.

Dinner was a semi-uncomfortable event. Over the meal Mychal told them a little about herself. The chancellor told her about the university and she learned about the area from Tony and Susanna. The uncomfortable part was Richard. His whole presence was rigid and brooding. He offered very little in terms of conversation and seemed to watch her intensely every time Mychal spoke.

After dinner, she was invited to the

music room to hear Susanna play a piano piece she had been working on. She declined saying she had unpacking to do; only to hear that the house aide, Alicia, unpacked her clothing during dinner. Mychal thought to herself 'oh, a house aide unpacked items during dinner, how uncultured of the guest not to know'. However, her boxes of personal things still remained unpacked. Mychal declined again saying she would like to get all the unpacking out of the way. So goodnights were said and she went upstairs while the others went their way to the music room.

Quietly, she entered the room and was greeted by a teenage girl straightening up Mychal's bed. Suddenly, she looked up and smiled. *"Hola, me llamo Alicia.* If you need me just call the number 11 on the house intercom system."

"Sí y me llamo Mychal Ayscue. Thank you for putting my things away. *Muchas Gracías."*

"*De nada.* It is my job. What should I do with those boxes?" she pointed to the living room. Then she pointed to the boxes in the bedroom, "*Y estos?*"

"Just leave them. Alicia can you show me how the intercom works *por favor*?" The young girl explained how to call different rooms in the house. She rattled off the numbers of some other rooms that Mychal was sure she would not remember later. This whole place was like living in a hotel suite. Who has room service and servants on hand in a house?

"*Gracias* again. I can finished here, so you can have the rest of your night. I'll say *buenos noches.*" Mychal really wanted to be alone.

"*Sí señora. Buenos noches,*" and the young girl left.

Mychal inspected her clothing arrangement before making a few changes to set things up a little closer to what she

had at home. Lastly, she checked her
makeup case and its contents under the
false bottom. Still locked, she slid it back
under the vanity. Next, she went to work
making the suite reflect her personality.

Dressed in grey running shorts and a
UNC Tarheels t-shirt, Mychal surveyed her
living room. The balcony doors were open
allowing a nice breeze to circulate the room.
The left door almost touched the tall
wooden clock in the corner. There were a
couple of house plants, a micro bar with
mini refrigerator, sofa, chair, end table and
wall mounted TV. With a sigh she began
the task of making the room more like her
home for the next year. Over an hour later,
she stood in the middle of the room
satisfied with the changes.

Behind the small area bar in the living
room hung an LED sign she and her older
brother swiped from Mardi Gras the year
before he got married. In the single chair
Mychal placed her large purple stuffed
gorilla, a souvenir from a trip to Las Vegas

with her younger brother. The coffee table and end table were littered with pictures of her family. Beside the right balcony door she hung a vampire facemask with her shades, a memento from the only Halloween party she and her sister ever attended which was before she married the jerk. The Vamps and Tramps party was scary fun. On the bathroom door was a poster of a blueish purple dragon holding a sword, a parting gift from her nephews. The last thing she had to do was move one of the house plants over to the bar.

Just as she picked up the plant she upset the balance of the table and sent it crashing to the floor as well as her toes. CLANG! She let out a yelp of surprise and pain. She was easing her toes from under the table when the door burst open. She jumped and nearly dropped the plant.

"*Que está pasando aquí?*" Her hostile host burst through the door. He was still in dinner clothes with the exception of dinner jacket and shoes. His shirt was unbuttoned

39

almost to the waist, revealing a narrow sprinkling of black hair. His deep bronze face was flushed with adrenaline and his crown of black hair tousled. With sharp dark green eyes, Richard stared coldly at her.

"I. . . I was just moving something," Mychal took a deep breath, trying to regain her composure, "and the table fell when I picked up the plant."

"If you needed help, why did you not ask?" He sounded irritated.

"I didn't think I needed any help," she hoped her voice came off more strongly than she felt inside. She was as much caught off guard by the table falling on her toes as his fireman like entrance. A little over six feet with a wide receiver build, he was an imposing figure whose glaring made the whole room uncomfortable.

"Here, give me that plant," he all but snatched the foliage from her hands.

She sat down on the sofa to inspect her red toes. Thankfully nothing was broken. She looked up to find Richard staring at her. She smiled and repeated aloud, "Nothing broken."

He did not return her smile but asked, "Where would you like the table?"

"In the bedroom beside the closet."

He put the plant down and moved the table where she wanted it. When he returned, Richard looked around the room. He had to smile a little at the odd things in the room. A neon Mardi Gras sign, a stuffed ape with a baseball cap, a weird rubber mask wearing shades and a poster of a mystical purple dragon with a dagger. "Just what are you trying to do? Was this not, um, comfortable enough for your taste?"

"I'm trying to put that plant on the other side of the sofa and my wireless speaker tower in the corner."

41

"Why not move the sofa down and replace the plant and table with the speaker? Look," he then proceeded to show her his idea. Mychal stood by the balcony and let the man enact his plan. When Richard finished the sofa was moved down with the speaker beside it. The plant was on the bar.

"Happy?" She nodded, silently admitting the way he had put things was better than what she had in mind. "Then *buenos noches* doctor."

"Like you mean it," she mumbled.

"And what is that supposed to mean?" he snapped, whipping around and looking ready to pounce.

"***That*** is what I mean. You cannot even be civil enough not to snap at me over trying to make my living space more personable. Just because you don't want me here does not give you the right to act childish and bully me the way you have been through your actions and attitude. If you don't want me here just say something so that other arrangements can be made," she retorted.

"Childish? Bully? Civil? How do you think someone should react when a totally different person from what they expect walks in the door? I think that I was nice enough not to throw you out," he fumed.

"That would have been stupid and unfair to me knowing I have nowhere else to go. You act like this whole mix-up is somehow completely my fault," her voice was flat.

All Richard could think was that she had some nerve, but said, "Stupid and unfair? You are the one being a difficult woman and-"

"Is that it? This whole thing is about me shattering your image or your plans to have another drinking buddy? Well, if it helps, I am sorry. I don't know what I can do to make things right other than grow a pair. Right name, wrong gender, the story of my life. If I could, I would turn my life in a complete three hundred and sixty degree spin. This trip would have never happened and I would be home with my family right now. Not wondering if I have a place to live or if I will be ill-treated over the next year. But I can't turn back the hands of time. So tell me. Tell me what I can do to change the fact that you hired me for a job and I am personally not what you wanted?" She could not keep the distress out of her voice.

Richard turned away and ran his hand through his hair. He had not considered that she was displace from her home thousands of miles away. She made a valid point which made him feel like a villain. Facing her again he sighed, "No doctor, I am the one that is sorry. You are the one who moved your entire life for this opportunity. You are here now and nothing can change the situation. We hired you because you were the best candidate for the job, not because we thought you had a beard-" She let out a whoop of laughter, "What is funny? Did I say something that amused you?"

"You were expecting my older brother Max. He and I look alike, except he is taller and has a beard. Let me show you," Mychal picked up a picture of her and her brother from the coffee table and showed Richard.

He noticed how happy the two looked in the picture, in matching bowling uniforms. He chuckled a little, "You are right. That does look something like the man I thought applied for the job. But you are here now and things will work themselves out."

As Mychal put the picture back, he could not help but noticed her tone athletic frame clad in a t-shirt and running shorts which showed off well-proportioned dancer like legs. The dress at dinner earlier was nice but definitely did not do her body any justice. Richard turned before she could catch him admiring her figure. He closed the door as softly as he spoke his parting words, "Sleep well doctor."

Mychal smiled at the door after he left. Incident aside, the man actually attempted to make one moment in her stay tolerable. Hopefully it would not be the last.

3
Discovery and Despair

Mychal's second day in her new home was one of discovery. After a small breakfast of fruit on her terrace, she met Susanna in the library. The younger woman wanted to start the tour outside in the front of the property. They walked out onto the manicured grass, as she explained the local history of the fruit trees that lined the driveway and how they served a duel purpose for their family. As they continued to tour the grounds, Susanna showed her the gardens that Pedro spoke of driving up to the house. The flowers were so vivid, that Mychal's touch lingered on each one and their perfume hung in the air. Right in the middle of all the vibrant colored flowerbeds, there was a semi inground koi pond with abundant plants and a fountain. There were two stone benches set apart from the fountain. Mychal made a note of the area behind the water feature for later purposes.

As they rounded a group of hedges, Mychal found them at the back left corner of the pool area. She was looking at an Olympic sized pool with an area twice that size designed for entertaining, equipped with lounge chairs, tables, umbrellas, a built in fireplace and firepit. In addition to local foliage that reminded her of banana trees, the area included an outdoor kitchen, and bar attached to a fully furnished pool house. Susanna explained Richard updated the area for their mother as she did aquatic therapy after her accident. He wanted her and the family to have a place that was both useful and enjoyable. She admitted that she was secretly delighted when their father agreed to the renovations. Growing up, their backyard was littered with cherubim statues and animal shaped shrubs, which Susanna grew to think was both antiquated and odd. On the way through the outside oasis, she pointed out the closed off *suegra* or mother-in-law wing of the villa explaining her grandparents lived there when they were too old to live alone.

Next, they went to the longer side of the U shaped house where all the cars were housed. Susanna told her Richard had the Porsche set aside for the man he thought would be the new professor, but she could pick out the car she wanted to drive. There were a couple of luxury sedans and an SUV housed with the other four sports cars. The tour continued on through the utility room and butler's pantry, rather large and airy kitchen with bar stools and breakfast area, a full bathrooms and powder room, the family room, music room, dining hall sized dining room which also served as a grand room on occasion and Richard's study.

Susanna pointed out the housekeepers' lodgings through a window on their way up the back stairs. Once upstairs, they peered into all the family bedrooms and guest rooms. Susanna pointed out that Mychal's current lodgings were Richard's old room as he moved into their parents' suite last year after deciding to host the foreign exchange professor.

By the time the main house tour was over, it was late afternoon, the traditional siesta time. Susanna explained that they normally nap or would have observed an hour of relaxation time after lunch. But she added more modern people were moving away from the tradition. However, it was time for the younger woman to practice her instruments. In addition to the piano, Susanna was working on mastering woodwind and string instruments.

Michael wondered what did her host family do to live such an extravagant lifestyle. She really wished she had found the time to video chat with them before moving. It definitely would have avoided yesterday's drama. With the younger woman practicing downstairs, Mychal had some alone time for the afternoon. Thinking Susanna had the right idea to practice, she decided to work out a little. Changing clothes and grabbing her phone and equipment, she headed to the garden for the spot she fell in love with earlier.

Once she got into her routine with electronica dance music blasting in her ears, Mychal lost track of time. It was not until she took off her ear buds, that she took notice of the sun setting. She gathered her equipment and headed toward the house. Halfway around the pool she met Richard.

"Where have you been?" he demanded.

"In the garden working out."

"Well, while you were in the garden, we were looking everywhere for you. Why did you not tell someone where you were going?" His anger made his accent heavier than normal.

"I didn't know that constant adult supervision was required here," was her flippant answer. "Plus, you could have just called me on the phone."

Ignoring her logical answer that he did not think of, Richard replied, "No one here has that number yet. Besides, as long as you are here you are my responsibility. You will let someone know the next time you wonder off. *¿Comprenda?*"

"Yes warden," Mychal mumbled on her way past him. How dare he insinuate that she wondered off like some kind of child. Damn, he was so imposing!

Richard ignored her comment but took notice again of the woman walking past him. Sweat hung on her tone arms and abdomen, while she carried a small black case and set of bamboo sticks. Strapped across her back was a leather holster containing what Richard made out to be a sword. He could only marvel at who this woman was, now living in his house.

Mychal arrived at dinner with her hair still damp in a French braid. She wore a pale pink tunic and black capris. Dinner was great and the evening's conversation flowed smoothly. Richard was only chilly toward her, occasionally eyeing her warily. After dinner she declined to hang out with the family again. She went to her room to write letters to her nephews. Feeling alone, Mychal put on a jazz selection and went to bed early.

The next day, Susanna took Mychal to her office on campus. It was in a restored building that looked older on the outside, but was modernized on the inside. The administrative assistant was a graduate student filling in for the regular person. When Mychal asked about meeting the department chair, she received a shrug, her keys and a welcome folder.

Mychal's office was a moderate size

with the standard office furniture. She needed to overhaul the place with a few things and splash of color. Her assigned laptop was locked in her desk drawer. She tried to log on to the computer, but her credentials must not have been in the university's IT system. She opened her welcome folder and sat reading the faculty handbook while waiting for Susanna to return. There was a knock at the door.

"Come in."

An attractive blond in tight jeans and a tight shirt with cleavage barely in check opened the door. She smiled uneasy and asked, "Is Dr. Ayscue in?"

"Yes."

"Where is he?" she spoke near perfect English.

"You're looking at her. Let me guess, you too thought it was going to be a man? Sorry," Mychal just shrugged.

The blond placed her hands on her hips and pouted, "Just my luck. I was expecting a good looking man to seduce and he turns out to be a she. The department faculty will be surprised! Well anyway I am Consuela Sevilla de Alfumirano. Connie for short. My office is two doors down." The blond extended her hand.

"I am Mychal Ayscue and it is nice to meet you." She shook her hand.

"No rings. Good, now I have someone to go out for drinks with after work some days. Let me tell you, around here sometimes you will need a drink. And the local spots are where the single men hang out."

"Well, I don't know. From what I have seen the men in this country are very chauvinistic," Mychal sounded skeptical.

"Mychal," Susanna called.

"Down in room 214," she called back.

Susanna came to stand in the doorway. "Ready to go?"

"Hello Susanna."

"Oh, hello Connie. What are you doing here? *¿Ser entrometido?*" Susanna's voice had a sarcastic edge. Her whole demeanor was icy.

"I'm just fraternizing with the new faculty. By the way, are your brothers still single?" The other woman batted her lashes.

"Which one? You have dated both."

"Ricardo. He is the more serious minded. Not to mention handsome. Six feet, built like a soccer legend with those pouty lips and sexy dark green eyes." Connie wet her lips. Mychal thought if this was the type of woman Richard preferred, no wonder he did not seem to like her.

"You can ask him yourself at the annual university gala. I assume you are coming to the party." Susanna made a momentary wincing face.

"I would not miss a chance to flirt with your brothers." She turned to Mychal, "Wait until you see them in black tie."

"Well, see you then Connie. Come on Mychal." Susanna turned to her and mouthed 'hurry up'. "See you then."

Connie went back to her office with a wave. Mychal closed the door and began asking questions, "What were you two talking about? Why were you acting so put off toward her? And what university gala?"

"Connie dated Tony first, but he was too much of a *canella*. Then she dated Richard. He was not serious about her. She is an *arribista*. So you see, she just wants to be with a García-Torres brother and it does not matter which one. In all honesty, I have no love loss for that woman. Would you care to drive home?" Susanna threw her the keys.

Mychal waited until they were in the car to ask about the party.

"Every year my family throws a gala on the Friday before classes start. *Es una fiesta grande* and the university faculty and staff come. It is like a formal festive opening ceremony to start the university's academic year," Susanna explained.

"Well I am glad you told me now. What do people wear to this function? Is it a sit down dinner? Can I get some more details? It will take me a week to get ready for a grand party."

"Usually me too. I will help you before Friday. Could we please go faster? You must learn to drive like the rest of the people here. On the *autovías* people are expected to speed."

Mychal needed space. Her weekend went smoothly until minutes ago. As she sat in her living room on the phone listening to her oldest brother, her heart filled with despair. Someone saying they were the New York State Bureau of Investigation called her house and talked with their mother on Friday. To make matters even worse, her brother-in-law, Jake, had been asking both him and their mother about her financial holdings. It was not enough he got her into a mess, now he was trying to nose into her financial affairs too. She needed time to think. How she missed her cabin in the North Carolina mountains. At this point she would even welcome the drive. The open space always helped to clear her head.

Instead, she made her way to the garden. She went to the stone bench by the koi pond with the fountain. She sat alone with her legs crossed, head hung in defeat, watching the colorful fish and thinking what an easy and simple life. Right now, she longed for a simple life too. She was so deep in thought that she did not hear Richard coming up behind her. He put his hand on her shoulder to get her attention. Reflexively she looped his arm and applied pressure. With quick fluid movements, she controlled his arm while turning to face an unknown adversary. Richard let out a yelp of surprise and pain.

She looked at him, bent over and attempting to suppress a pained look and sternly said, "You should never sneak up on me. I could have really hurt you."

"You mean worse than now?" She really had him in a disadvantaged position.

Mychal released him with a pat on his arm, "A lot worse."

She eyed him suspiciously, "What are you doing here anyway? Were you following me? Sorry warden, I did not check out of the house again."

"Not exactly, I was leaving my study

when I heard someone walk by. I found you here, looking asleep. When I touched you, you almost broke my arm," Richard rubbed his forearm. "Where did you learn moves like that?"

"Self-defense class. Look, I'm sorry," Mychal muttered, feeling low. Richard was just being a concerned host.

"No harm. However, you should not be out here alone. It is late and dark."

"I just needed to be alone with my thoughts."

"I know you were on the phone earlier. I could hear you getting loud when I walked by your room. Was it your family? Is everything fine? Would you like to talk to someone? Is there something I can do to help?" He sounded as though he genuinely wanted to help her or just wanted her to talk to him. She looked distressed.

"My family is fine. I didn't realize I would miss home that much," Mychal lied.

She quickly wiped away the tear that escaped her eye.

"Please doctor, do not-" he tried.

"I'm not crying!"

"All right then. Do not let drops of salt water leak from your eyes!" She turned to give him a weak smile then burst into giggles. Puzzled he said, "I did not think my joke was that funny."

"No, Richard, it's you. Wait, before you say anything let me explain. You are attempting to be nice to me. I didn't think you had a nice side and matching sense of humor. You are always so grim and condemning to me. Always the warden, making the stay with the host family safe but unpleasant. It was surprising to hear you make an actual joke," she grinned at him.

"Well doctor. After I got over the initial shock and anger of you not being the person I imagined we hired for the position,

I decided to make the best of the situation. I thought I would try to be a better host or least something like a friend or housemate. We have to live under the same roof over the next year and there is no use in making it harder than it has to be. How does that sound?" He looked shyly.

"Like a good idea," she stuck out her hand for a confirming handshake. "Deal?"

He took it and placed a gentle kiss on the back. Still holding her hand he said, "Come on friend, or housemate or whatever, I will escort you to your room. I heard there was an arm breaking American ninja out on the grounds tonight. No one is safe."

Mychal chuckled and gave him a winning smile that warmed Richard's heart, "Now that we're friends, or housemates, or whatever, how about giving me a ride to work tomorrow? Or better yet, I will take you to work, that way I can get a feel for driving here," she explained.

"We will talk about that later."

"What about a tour of the city as my host family? You know the restaurants, museums, shopping, and best cultural spots. Or how about your office? Can we start there? What do you do anyway? Are you really a warden at a prison?"

Richard could only shake his head and smile. He rolled his dark green eyes at her rapid fire questions, "Later, later, you will be here a whole year. Am I going to regret being your friend, housemate or whatever?"

"Only if you fight it. Resistance is futile."

4

Friends and Attractions

Her second week in August felt like Mychal's real orientation to the American College of Madrid, starting with a university wide meeting on Monday. The next few days were spent on tours of campus, unit meetings, departmental meetings, and arranging her office. During this time, she met a fellow professor, Ruby Alcevez and her husband, Luis, who was one of the university's staff doctors. Thursday afternoon she was surprised by a visit from Richard during siesta time.

"Hello doctor," he stood in her doorway dressed in black slacks and a white pin stripe shirt with a fashionable tie. He moved into her office and sat in a chair.

"Well, if it isn't the chairman of the board as well as my new friend slash housemate. What do I owe the pleasure of this visit today?" She asked, putting down the syllabus she had been working on.

"First, as the head of your host family, I wanted to tell you to make time for a physical with one of the university doctors. Then, I wanted to make an appointment with you for tomorrow. I thought we would go on that tour I promised."

"That's nice Richard, but you could have asked me at home. You do live down the hall."

"Yes, but I wanted to make sure I did it officially and hopefully before your day filled up with other appointments. I also wanted to know how you were getting along at work so far. You look busy doing professor stuff." Richard quickly surveyed her surroundings. Her office was a little cluttered but bearable. She had some posters and artwork on the walls as well as pictures of her family. It was nothing compared to her suite back at the house.

"I guess a day with the chairman and head of my host family is a reasonable excuse to sneak away," Mychal smiled at the idea.

"Of course, it is strictly business," Richard smiled too at the irony of the idea. He rose to leave.

"Where are you going? I thought you came by for a while," she frowned.

"Yes, for a short while. I have to visit Uncle Juan to discuss some upcoming university gala business before the next board meeting. I will be back before it is time to go if you want me to show you another route home."

"That's fine, but," she could not resist this moment, "I thought maybe you would like to wait and speak to Connie before you go. Her office is just a couple of doors down the hall."

Richard made a face as though sucking on sour candy, "You have met her?"

"Oh yes, and she seemed so fond of you," Mychal teased.

"Let me go before she knows I am here. And you cannot tell her I was here either," he gave her a conspirator's wink.

"You better leave then because I think I smell her perfume coming this way," she laughed as he waved and shot out the door.

Mid Friday morning, Richard began their tour with a visit to *The Prado*. Mychal saw a few Goya and Italian paintings and was ready to go, much to Richard's dismay. Next, they went to the *Plaza de España* to see the statues of Don Quixote and Sancho Panza. She made the comment that the statues reminded her of the ones in the city. Mychal seemed to enjoy that so much that he took her to the *Plaza de Cibeles* to see the statue of Cybele, the Greek goddess of fertility and protection. They stopped for lunch at a cafe in the plaza.

During lunch, Richard told Mychal a little history of Madrid, as well as a little about himself. He told her that his parents had him in their mid-thirties and his other siblings a few years short of fifty. His mother was paralyzed in a plane crash while he was in college in America. He came home to help care for his mother, knowing his father struggled with seeing his wife in a disabled state. A year after his mother's accident and upon his father's insistence, he went back to the West Miami University to complete his degree in business.

He was in his second year of graduate school when his father decided that he was too old to handle the family businesses. He wanted to care for his wife full time. Richard returned home to become the company president and handle all the subsidiary companies. His father stayed on as a company consultant until his mother's death. His father passed away within months. Then, not only was he company president, but also served in his father's board positions in certain establishments as well. That was five years ago and the reason he was chairman of the university board at his age. Mychal felt touched that he shared so much with her. It somehow made their day more personal than business.

Next, they stopped at the Royal Palace for a short time. Knowing that Mychal did not enjoy museums, Richard only walked around the front of the palace giving her its rich history. Thinking Mychal would enjoy seeing an older part of Madrid, they went to the *Plaza Mayor*. He could only smile as she marveled over the history of the bullfights. He could feel her delight as she dragged him by the hand from churches to squares to shops. He surprised her with the next stop; a visit to the Bullfighting

Museum. Her excitement was like that of a kid in a candy store. The final stop on their tour was the major crossroads of Spain, *Puerta del Sol*. There, they had dinner while enjoying the view of Madrid's night life. Arriving home after midnight, Richard suggested to a tired Mychal to sleep in the next day, as he had no plans for anything special for her. On Sunday they were going to have a family outing at one of the local parks.

Sunday could not have been a more beautiful day. Richard had Pedro's wife pack an enormous wicker basket with food for a dozen people. She, Richard and Susanna rode together while Tony rode with his new female friend. Upon arrival, they picked a nice spot by a shade tree. The guys kicked around a soccer ball while Susanna and Mychal laid out the food. Tony's new girlfriend, Mychal soon discovered, was a bit ditzy and spent her time cheering whenever Tony's foot touched the ball.

71

After the meal, Tony and the ditzy girlfriend went off walking while Richard took a nap on the blanket, leaving Mychal and Susanna talking about western culture. They discussed things ranging from how American education systems fail to bring the arts to every child in public schools to the double standards of equality. They talked about the differences in how they were raised. Although Mychal was from a blended family, they did not quite get the dynamics of the blending correct. She too had two brothers with her oldest brother being the one they looked to for guidance.

Susanna talked about how their parents purposely worked to make their children close despite the age difference. Though Richard was twelve years older than she and Tony, they always did family things to forge close bonds. When Richard stepped into the family guidance role after their father passed, he took his commitment super serious. Sometimes he forgot he was her brother and not their father. He still treated Susanna like a teenager.

When Richard woke up, he took Mychal on a short trip to *San Francisco el Grande*. Although they spent much of the weekend together, Mychal did not remember Richard holding her hand the way he did in the church. He seemed totally at ease with her now. She caught him looking at her strangely a few times but when she asked what was wrong, he just smiled and said nothing.

With the visit ending, they returned to the picnic area. Susanna, who was close playing with some children, acknowledged their return with a wave. It was Mychal's turn to take a nap, but Richard wanted to read, so he fought her for the best spot on the blanket. He won, so she slept beside him.

She was awakened by the gentle stroking of her face. She opened her eyes to see Richard's face hovering above hers seconds before his lips brushed her cheek.

Mychal didn't know if it was a kiss or a mistake. He whispered in her ear, accent thicker than usual, "Time to go *la bella durmiente del*."

She was still groggy as he helped pull her to her feet so he could fold the blanket while Susanna packed up the picnic items. During the car ride she dozed off again. By the time they reached home she was slowly coming awake. It was still early and Mychal wanted something to do. Susanna suggested they call their neighbor Rafael for a light dinner of lunch leftovers and a game of cards. When Mychal met Rafael, she thought he was more of a playboy than Tony. Susanna reminded their neighbor of the party on Friday. He responded he would be there with a family member that was staying in town. The night was well spent with laughter and wine. Mychal went to bed and fell asleep immediately.

That Monday, the same Monday before classes started it rained. Ignoring the dress code, Mychal went to work in jeans, sneakers, t-shirt and baseball cap. That afternoon, she went for her physical with none other than Luis Alcevez. Mychal really took to him. He was like a funny uncle at the holidays, always joking and lovable. Although he looked like a retired city bus driver, slightly overweight and hair a complete white halo, his big hands were surprisingly gentle. The next three days she had more meetings, met new people including some eager students and worked on her syllabi. All day Friday was spent in preparation for the university party.

By Friday, however, Mychal had mixed feelings about the university gala. She wanted school to start and this party would signal that. Yet, she was very hesitant. She was getting to know her host family, but would she fit into their social group? She still did not know what to wear to such a staff party. She laid out three party dresses, polished her nails and napped on the sofa.

She was awaken by Susanna shaking

her, "Get up! I have been calling your room with no answer. Does your intercom work? You are going to be late for the party."

"Okay. I'll be ready in twenty minutes. No wait. Which dress?" Susanna pointed to the black one.

In less than twenty minutes Mychal was ready. She slipped into the low cut black sequined dress and put her hair in a chignon. From her makeup case she extracted diamond and white gold teardrop earrings with a matching necklace. Lastly, she put on light makeup then made her way downstairs.

Rafael, the card playing playboy neighbor, saw her first. He looked like a cross between a male college cheerleader and some infamous spy. The white dinner jacket against his golden skin gave him an exotic appearance. Beside him was a distinguishably handsome short wiry gentlemen with a deep tan. "My darling Mychal, you look marvelous."

"Thank you. You too."

"Mychal this is my Uncle Mato. Uncle Mato this is the new foreign exchange professor at the university," Rafael introduced them.

"It is a pleasure to meet you Uncle Mato. If it is okay for me to call you that?" She extended her hand.

"Amato Delossantos and the pleasure is all mine," he took her hand and kissed it. His accent was hard to place, but his English was perfect. "You can call me Uncle Mato if you are as comfortable as I am with it."

"Thank you, Uncle Mato. What do you do, I mean what kind a business are you in?" Mychal made light conversation.

"Importing and exporting trades mostly." The older man smiled easily. He was so stately and polished, that Mychal thought he could have been a politician. She bet in his younger days, he was quite the charmer.

She flashed him a winning smile, "Well, I am glad you could make it to this gala."

"As am I. I was hoping to chat with your host a little more about business in the area. I am considering going into the shipping business here in Spain."

Mychal knew his accent sounded different from the locals. "You are not from the area?"

"No my dear, I live in Athens. My family including, Rafael's mother, is from Greece. My sister moved here to pursue a career in medical research. She married another researcher and settled here. I come to see my nephew every so often to keep him on the right path," Uncle Mato clapped Rafael on the back.

She smiled at his affectionate gesture and joked, "He might need it at this party."

"Indeed."

"Thanks Uncle Mato. Mychal, please, let me escort you," he linked his arm in hers. Leaving his uncle they headed toward the grand room. Together they turned heads until Richard spotted her. Immediately, he made his way toward her.

"Rafael." Though speaking to his neighbor, his gaze traveled from Mychal's face to the cleavage shown by the low cut to her curvaceous legs exposed by the split in her dress. "Hello my good doctor, you look stunning. Please come with me. We have been waiting for you."

Mychal blushed as he snaked an arm around her waist and walked them away from Rafael.

When they walked into the grand room, Richard got everyone's attention. He spoke when the room quieted, "Good evening and welcome to our annual faculty gala. This year we have a guest of honor:

our foreign exchange professor, Dr. Mychal Ayscue. Dr. Ayscue is from America and will be staying the academic year. She is located in the English literature department for those who do not know her field."

When they applauded, she felt compelled to give a response, "Thank you for the warm introduction. I hope that this year will be prosperous for the university."

"*Graçias*. I hope so as well doctor. ¡ *Vamos A comer!*" Richard led Mychal to one of the bistro style dining tables littered throughout the library, formal living room, dining room and music room.

Dinner was pleasant. Food and drink flowed as well as bilingual conversation, which jumped from subject to subject. Mychal was caught up in all this and drank slightly too much. When the party returned to the grand room for dancing, she was ready to join the festivities. She danced frequently to American and Spanish music. She danced with the people she knew like Luis, Ruby, Rafael, his Uncle Mato, and Tony. When she attempted to take a break, Richard pulled her onto the dance floor. The song had a slow cultural rhythm.

"What's wrong with you?" he angrily hissed in her ear, accent heavier due to irritation. "I do not want people to think my new foreign exchange professor is somewhat of an over the top party girl."

She giggled at him, "You're just being silly. I'm grown and having a good time."

Richard's dark green eyes narrowed to slits. "You are very drunk!"

"Please. This is not me being very drunk at all."

"Come on. You need some air," with a firm grip, he started to lead her out to the pool when a hand grabbed his arm.

"Quickly Richard! There is something that requires your attention."

"You stay here!" Richard punctuated every word as the other man almost dragged him away. As he left, Mychal had to admit Connie was right because Richard was very attractive in black tie.

Mychal wandered to her favorite place in the garden, the koi pond. She sat on the bench and slipped off her shoes. She closed her eyes listening to the music from the party. A noise behind her brought her senses to full alert.

"Mychal is that you?" Rafael came up behind her.

"Yes, Rafael."

"You look wonderful tonight. I kept trying to get you alone all night, but everyone wanted your attention." His hands massaged her shoulders.

She did not reply to him, wondering why in the hell he was even out here.

"It is a lovely and romantic picture; you

and I alone in the garden. This whole scenario does something to me." He slipped a strap off her shoulder and began kissing her bare skin. His hands moved lower dipping into the front of her dress.

His move snapped Mychal out of her daze. She locked both arms around his neck and flung Rafael over her shoulder with practiced ease. He put out his hands in anticipation to fend off the expectation of punches, but miscalculated. Just as one of his hands hit her face, she delivered a single blow to his groin. Rafael howled in pain. Mychal staggered to her feet. "Oh, shut up!"

She picked up her sandals and turning to leave bumped into Tony. His arms shot out to steady her as she drew back to punch.

"Hold on. I'm a friend. What's happening out here?"

"Nothing," she snapped, fixing her

strap.

"Nothing," Rafael echoed getting up slowly and painfully. "Just a small misunderstanding."

"I hope so. Rafael, I think you have had too much to drink. Your uncle left a few minutes ago and perhaps you should go home too. You know the way out. Come on Mychal. Let's go to the house."

Leaving his neighbor to see himself out, Tony draped an arm around her shoulders and escorted her to the house. As they came closer, he turned and said, "I think you should freshen up. Richard sent me outside to your favorite spot to see how you felt after a moment of fresh air. He has someone he wants you to meet."

When she got inside, Mychal went to the bathroom. The image in the mirror was terrible. Her hair was loose from the chignon, her face was flushed and worst of all her bottom lip was bleeding. She frowned as she wiped the blood away. Then she pulled the pins out of her hair, fingered it to partially hide her face and left the room. Tony was waiting for her.

"Come on. You are just going to love Richard's surprise guest."

The minute they walked in the grand room Richard spotted her. He and a stunningly attractive brunette walked toward her. The other woman wore a semi sheer nude gown with a plunging neckline that was less than inches away from the front split in the dress. Her makeup was clearly professionally done. She eyed Tony and the newcomer with veiled interest. "Mychal, this is Demitri Salvos. She is one of our family's friends. Demitri this is our exchange professor, Dr. Mychal Ayscue."

The woman looked Mychal up and down. "Lovely dress. It is similar to one of the originals I own."

"What a pleasure it is to meet you. I'm

glad to hear we have similar taste. Great minds often think alike," Mychal put on her best sickening sweet, over-the-top girlfriend routine, not caring if she sounded the slightest bit petty or rude. At the moment, being sociable was the furthest thing from her mind. Richard gave her a sharp look.

"How has your stay been?"

"Good, thank you for asking. I have a wonderful host family."

"I know," the other woman smiled at Richard. "He is a wonderful man."

Catching the other woman's hint and tired of conversation, Mychal pleaded fatigue and went to her room. Once in her room, she shed the dress and hopped in the shower. She was sitting on her bed, dressed in a paisley chemise and matching robe, talking to Alicia on the phone when Richard walked in without so much as a knock. He sat on the bed as she hung up.

He spoke in a low controlled voice, "Why did you not tell me what happened tonight?"

"Because, it was not important and I took care of it. Besides you were a wonderful host. You were making sure people had a great time. That was your job not only as chairman of the board but also as the proprietor." She added with a lazy intoxicated smile, "By the way, the party was great."

"That was not half as important as what happened to you. You were attacked tonight. I have known Rafael for years and never thought him capable of this. You could have been seriously hurt. I should have been told immediately," Richard shook his head in disbelief.

Mychal rolled her eyes, "I was not attacked and there was no harm done. If you want to worry about someone, try Rafael. He got a little overzealous and I taught him a lesson. Really, Richard! You are making something out of nothing."

He cupped her face and grazed her split lip with his thumb, "Is this nothing as well?"

"I have had worse. Like concussion worse. "

"But not on my watch." He gave her a lopsided grin. Impulsively he teased, "I will kiss it and make it better."

He did with a gentle peck that produced an awkward moment. Ignoring the prickly pain from her lip and encouraged by the alcohol she consumed, Mychal's hands snaked into his ebony locks, and pulled him into a deeper kiss. Her tongue tasted his, making him want more than an intoxicated kiss. His lips left her mouth and went to the scented curve of her neck. When he pulled her closer, his hands felt her soft feminine curves, covered only by a thin layer of satin. Her body felt so good, so warm. It held such potential to warm his empty heart. Knowing this simple act could get out of hand, he did not want to scare her off with any regrettable actions. Her alcohol fueled kiss had indeed caught him off guard. She was kissing his ear shaking his own intoxicated reserve.

The knock at the door gave Richard a reason to stop. He straightened up his appearance and looked at a still glowing Mychal. When she too had straightened up, he called for entrance. Alicia came in with some ice. She whispered something in Spanish to Richard then left.

"Okay, here is some ice. Into bed with you."

"Promise?" She teased.

"Mychal, *portarse bien,*" he warned.

Mychal disrobed and the sight of her in that short gown made Richard swallow hard. She slid between the sheets knowing Richard's eyes were on her. He placed the cold compress on her lip while whispering 'goodnight'. He traced the outline of her face with his finger while she winked back at him. He took a deep breath to secure his control before leaving the room.

Richard returned to the winding down party. Being the gracious host, he made sure everybody had a safe method to get home. When everyone left, Richard, Tony and Susanna helped the housekeepers close things down. At 6:00 am, Richard started upstairs to bed. Quietly, he slipped into Mychal's room to check on her. She was sleeping soundly. She had thrown the covers off sometime during the night and now lay on her stomach, short chemise exposing her round, tone bottom. Her lip was swollen and her face was covered in a light sweat.

Silently, he walked over and pulled the sheet up. Then he turned the ceiling fan on low. He let his gaze linger a minute longer. When she first walked in the door all Richard could see was a bad situation. However, he did not miss the fact she was a strong, beautiful woman. Richard eased out the room and down the hall to his own room.

To his surprise Demitri lay asleep in his bed. There were two wine glasses on the night stand and she wore a sexy negligee. Richard frowned and mumbled something like 'nice try, but not on your best day.' He picked up his pajama pants from the sofa and went to sleep in one of the guest rooms.

5

Dates and Exes

It was late when Mychal got up. She
had a killer headache, an ugly swollen lip
and pieces of last night's bad decisions
floating in her head. After some aspirin
and a hot bath, she began her traditional
weekend before school activities. Her run
was somewhat revealing. The neighboring
villas were stunning. Many looked older
than the one she was currently residing in,
some looked newer. Each had its own
distinct style. Some had fountains in front,
some had long peach tree lined drive ways,
and some of the newer ones had tennis and
basketball courts. One she saw had its own
mini soccer field. Many were behind

private entrances with massive gates. The country side was something to behold. From the road she could see lush greenery with the roof tops of villas nestled in. Everything seemed so . . . peaceful. There was some traffic on the road, but it was not like the noisy traffic of New York. After her run, she went upstairs to retrieve her workout weapons and phone, just in case she 'wondered off' again. She spent the remaining daylight hours in her favorite garden spot working out.

The evening was Mychal's pampering time. Time to clean up and go out. She was on her way downstairs when she met Richard.

"Wow, you look nice," he noticed how she really seemed to glow. "Special date?"

"No, just treating myself before the semester starts."

"I cannot let a beautiful woman like you go out alone in the city. Please, let me take you out," he smiled gingerly. She was dazzling in a deep purple maxi dress and sand colored wedge sandals.

Mychal thought about it. Did she want to continue her evening alone or spend some time building better bridges with Richard? Meaning better bridges than a misunderstood drunk kiss. "Well, I wasn't going anywhere fancy, just a little restaurant near the campus. You can go on one condition, it has to be my treat. Okay?"

"I cannot let you do that. I am your host remember?" She shook her head negatively to his response. "No? *Bien*, but first we must *tapear*, my treat. I need to change."

Her look gave him the once over. Long legs in smug fitting blue khakis, loafers, and a white polo shirt covering broad shoulders and tapered waist, black hair somewhere between tousled and needing to be combed. Yeah, he could definitely go with her. Mychal unconsciously licked her lips. "I do not know what *tapear* is, but I think you're fine."

"Great, let me close my study and we are off."

Going from bar to bar eating *tapa* or hors d'oeuvres was like festivals in the city to Mychal. The blend of various foods, wines, and people was great. The restaurant she chose was small and comfortable. Their table was outside on a cobbled area. While drinking after dinner wine, Richard wanted to ask questions about her life back at home.

"You are such a reserved, yet professional woman. There are so many things I want to know about you." With her nod of permission he began, "Let's start with your name. While it is a common name for men, how did you get that name with an unusual spelling?"

"My godfather. My godparents didn't have any kids. When I was born my mother named me after him. The spelling was her way of attempting to make it look feminine on paper."

"Your accent sounds like you lived in New York all your life. Am I right?"

"Yes,. Born and raised in the Bronx," she sipped her wine.

"I saw all of your pictures of family the night you moved in. Other than your brother, do you have other siblings?"

"Yes. Max and I are the older set of siblings. Then there is my brother Reese and sister Riley," Mychal made an effort not to roll her eyes. "My mother was married to their father for most of my childhood."

"Has it been tough for you being a successful career woman? The women I have dealt with in business always complain about the glass ceiling for women in America," he leaned forward with his elbows on the table.

"Not really." Mychal gave him a warming smile, "But if I were in a super competitive field maybe so. In academia, you are only competing against yourself and where you want your career to go. Everything is about publishing, presenting and research. To be honest, I didn't expect to get as far as I have. I was lucky, I had a great set of mentors who included me in their academic endeavors which compelled my career. Every new accomplishment in my life is almost like a surprise to me. So if there was a glass ceiling, I didn't feel the effects."

"You seem to have done well with your career. Surely your personal life has suffered? A career decision in which you had to leave your friends, family, and companion must have been hard. I feel sorry for the guy you left back in the States. You are a wonderful woman," Richard was subconsciously fishing.

"You don't know that," she said without looking up. He was trying to reach out to her and she had to put up a barrier concerning her past. Feeling guilty, she went on cautiously, "I stayed busy back in New York. Between traveling for presentations, writing and other tenure and promotion activities, I never had time for a serious relationship. My family was all I needed."

"Do not kid me. Not even in college?"

"Especially not in college. I tried to date, but it never worked out. Working full time and carrying a full course load in school does not leave much time to have a relationship. I did martial arts tournaments with my school's competition team and wanted to party with what free time I had left. Plus, I went to college with the weight of my family on my shoulders. They sacrificed everything for me to go to college while my brother was attending at the same time. Max and I were only born two years apart. I, no we, could not disappoint them."

"And . . . "

"And I didn't, no *we* didn't. He went to law school. I graduated early and went straight through for my masters and doctorate. Same thing as now except there was research. Lots and lots of research. Graduated, got a job and wrote the book." Richard sighed catching Mychal off guard. "What was that for?"

"I wish I knew you then. You sounded like a beautiful driven martial arts nerd."

She chuckled with relief, "Richard that was a long time ago filled with days of, like I said lots of research. Think of the now; I am here with my new host family and new things to do with them. Don't remorse over things in my self-imposed sheltered nerd past, look forward to the things we will do as my family away from home."

"You are right," he changed the subject, "Would you like to go dancing?"

They left and went to a local club. The

people, the colors and the music captivated Mychal so much she did not want to dance. When a soft melody began to play, Richard lured Mychal onto the dance floor. He moved slowly to the beat with her body inches away from his.

"Doctor, I have a confession to make," he spoke softly, "I think I am beginning to like you."

"Of course you are. We finally got over 'she's not a guy', I live in your house and I drive your Porsche. Plus, at some point, I think we decided to be friends," she said sarcastically.

"No, not like that. Like this," he gave her a searing kiss that ignited her senses. He pulled her body to mold his own as his tongue played games with hers.

She mumbled against his mouth, "Richard, this is not the place for that."

He whisked her outside to a small verandah. Then he kissed her again, this

time caressing her curves lightly. "*¡Dios
mío!* You feel so good next to me. Your
touch does something to me every time. I
just cannot explain it. *¡Me deja hacer el amor
contigo.*"

How could she deny something that
felt so . . . so undeniable. She was so
recklessly attracted to him that even his
smoldering looks sent vibes throughout her
body. Oh, yes she did want him to touch
her in places that where long abandoned by
her last boyfriend. Mychal's imagination
would not let her go there. Hell, she just
met the man less than a month ago. She
would handle this before anything got out
of hand. "Richard, this is my fault. Last
night, things got out of hand. I don't want
you to get the wrong idea."

He pulled back to look at her, but did
not let her go, "Meaning?"

"I was maybe, kind of drunk last night.
I was on an adrenaline rush from that thing
with Rafael and you were in the wrong

place at the wrong time. I sort of pounced on you and I'm sorry if you got the wrong idea."

Richard watched her flounder with her explanation, trying not to smile. He took a breath and said, "What if I am not sorry?"

"What?"

"What if I liked what happened last night and want it to happen again? I was a willing participant who will encourage it to happen even more." He kissed her again, this time with urgency to let her know he meant what he said.

Mychal's body responded as her mind digested his words before the kiss. He maneuvered her hips to caress her round bottom and brush against his thighs. Her head was spinning as things were moving way too fast. She broke their kiss, "It's late Richard. Time to go home."

Although they were like two anxious teenagers in the car, kissing and touching, they made it home safely. Together, they were about to go outside to the garden for more alone time.

"Richard, where have you been?" Demitri's voice hit them like cold water from the top of the stairs. She came down the stairs dressed in a negligee covered by a thin silk robe. "I have been so worried. You did not answer my calls or texts. Never mind all that. You must be tired after being out all night. Thank you for bringing my Richard home. Now, come to bed."

Richard looked at Mychal irritated, "*Buenos noches* doctor. We will have to do this again sometime. I had a great time."

Then he shook his head and mouthed, 'this is not over' and 'not what you think.'

"Goodnight Richard," her nonverbal response was a wink. Once in her room Mychal had to laugh in spite of things. The whole situation reminded her of teenagers

getting caught by somebody's mother. Yet
she was glad that things had not gone any
further. Not yet anyway, according to him.
Nothing worse than making a mistake and
having to live with it for the rest of the
academic year. Mychal had to shake her
head in wonder. How did things go from
them fighting as soon as she walked in the
door to a drunk kiss to going out and
kissing while they danced? She was on a
slippery slope wearing skis.

The next morning Susanna awakened
her for a late breakfast. With little
enthusiasm Mychal slipped on yoga pants
and a Carolina Panthers t-shirt, washed her
face and went downstairs. Tony gave her a
conspirator's smile and wink and everyone
bid her *buenos días*. Mychal just frowned.
What did he know that she did not?
Midway through the meal Susanna said,
"You are so quiet today. What is wrong?"

"I don't agree with mornings,
especially this morning."

"Perhaps it was your late hours. A woman, especially a foreigner, should not be out so late in the city. At least Richard was there to keep you from any harm." Demitri murmured, "Such a gentlemen."

"Perhaps," Mychal muttered in return. For that she received a kick under the table from Susanna.

"Richard was up late as well. When I got home this morning, he wanted to talk a hole in my head." Tony chimed in, "I was wondering why he was downstairs in his office."

Once breakfast was over Mychal headed back to bed. Before she could, Susanna came asking questions with one knock at the door.

"What did she mean by that? What happened last night and what are you not telling me?"

Mychal sat in bed and recounted last night's events. When she finished the younger woman looked amazed, "She has got some nerve. So are you and my brother going out again today? Another date?"

"Date? No, no, no. We were not out on a date last night. Today is my day to rest. Maybe I will relax by the pool for an afternoon nap."

Susanna rose to leave, "Well, come get me when you are ready to go out."

That afternoon was spent by the pool with Susanna. Mychal worked on her tan in a teal and red bikini. A while later, they were joined by Tony, then Richard and Demitri. The two women were in deep conversation when Demitri arrived.

"Ladies," she greeted them dressed in a green string bikini that left no guess work. "Mychal do you feel any better from this morning?"

"I did until moments ago. Thanks for asking." Mychal was beginning not to like Richard's Demitri Salvos. For some unknown reason, she just rubbed Mychal the wrong way. She turned back to Susanna, dismissing the other woman. "Your trip really does sound wonderful."

"I know and Tony is going with some new girl. I just hope Richard will permit me to go."

Mychal replied somewhat astonished, "Let you go? Honey you are twenty-three years old and still getting permission to take overnight trips? He is your brother, right?"

"Yes," Susanna quietly replied.

"You see Dr. Ayscue," Demitri interrupted, "women of proper cultivation and formal schooling in this country must still ask the family patron when something she wants to do may seem risqué or bring shame to the family name. American women who were raised in broken homes or do not have a husband do not understand that cultural concept."

She paused, then said, "Western women are so brusque and recklessly independent. Very few have proper schooling and correct rearing."

Mychal just could not let that shot pass. Those once unknown reasons why she did not like Demitri were making themselves known. She sighed and replied as if it bothered her to actually speak to the other woman, "Demitri, that was a culturally insensitive and stereotypical comment. You sound kind of like an American bigot."

The other woman appeared unfazed by the insult, "It is just that the western women I have met on tour have some tragic upbringing and are desperately single."

"It's a shame that you would make such a comment based on a limited view of women in America," Mychal could not keep the loathing out of her voice. "If you think so little of western women, why do you try to emulate them? I noticed that you have on the same swimwear as the model on the cover of that magazine under your towel?"

Red and flustered, Demitri replied, "I . . . I was reading it for the interesting western articles."

"Yeah, sure," Mychal sneered. Then she turned to Susanna, "When is your brother going to realize you are not a child? It amazes me how you and Tony are twins and he treats you totally different in many ways. When will he realize that you both are adults and should be treated as such? You should talk to him. Really talk to him."

"I do not know if that will help. But I think that talk might have to be someday soon," Susanna looked distant.

6
Bullies and Apologies

The week began without mishaps. English classes in Madrid were different and between some of their accents and hers made communication a little strained the first few days. The following week was somewhat better. She was asked to join a committee revising curricula. Friday night after organizing work for the next week, Mychal was ready to hit the bed. After spending hours modifying her syllabi to include some online assignments in every course then adding those assignments in the online learning platform, she left a trail of clothes from the sofa in the living room to the bed. She had planned to sleep until

Saturday afternoon.

However, she was awakened by the overhead light in her room. She opened one eye to see Richard staring at her, looking like a cross between worried and angry. She reached down and pulled up the sheet to cover her body dressed in only a tank and bikinis. To block him out even more, she put a pillow over her head. "Go away. I am tired. Unless there is death, hell or destruction, just go away."

"Mychal, are you listening? Susanna is missing. She is not home and her bed has not been slept in."

"So go ask Tony where she is," she replied without removing the pillow from her head.

"He is out for the evening. Susanna should have been home by now."

"And?" Mychal asked a little annoyed, now pulling the covers over the pillow.

"And I am worried. I want you to go with me to find her." Now Richard was getting annoyed.

Mychal sat up and tucked the sheet under her arms, "Richard, you woke me up at the ass crack of dawn otherwise known as zero dark thirty on a Saturday morning because Susanna is not home and Tony is still out. Then, you want me to help you find her. Where? Please, go away and let me sleep."

"I know Tony can take care of himself but Susanna is not old enough to-"

She cut him off snapping out, "I don't want to hear it! Just get out and I will get dressed to help you especially if it means I can get back to sleep while it is still dark."

Slowly, she threw on a yoga outfit and pulled her hair in a ponytail. Mychal heard drawers slamming shut and went down the hall past Richard's and Tony's to Susanna's bedroom. She saw Richard on Susanna's bed raffling through a notebook.

"What the hell are you doing?"

"Trying to call that Alejandro guy she brought to the party. If he is not home, she is out with him," he grumbled.

"Stop being foolish and come on," Mychal rolled her eyes and stomped away down the back staircase.

He caught up with her in the garage. Mychal was leaning against Tony's red Aston Martin, "I thought you said he was out."

"He is. He went with some friends to the beach this weekend."

Suddenly Mychal remembered, "That's where she is! Susanna said she was thinking of going, but wanted to talk with you first."

Richard snapped, "Well, she did not! Now she is gone! Why did you not come and tell me?"

"I just remembered. And what do you mean 'why didn't I tell you'? She wanted to handle this like an adult and to talk to you. I thought she did." Mychal walked away saying, "Besides, she is with Tony. If he's okay, she's okay."

Richard snagged her arm before Mychal got to the first step to the house. "Look Mychal Ayscue, I do not know what you consider adult age, but Susanna is not old enough to go off on weekends in this household. She did this to defy me and you helped her by not saying anything."

Mychal's eyes narrowed to slits as her stare bore into Richard. "I didn't help her do anything. This problem was here long before I came. You treat her as a child and treat her twin the exact opposite. You constantly demean her with your attitude. What I did was listen to a very excited young woman tell me her possible plans for the weekend. As for me not telling you, I don't think personal snitch was in the job description. Susanna said she would talk with you and I believed her."

Richard glared back.

"Now," she hissed through clenched teeth, eyes glowing amber daggers, "release my arm."

Snatching her arm out of his grasp with no resistance she stomped away.

Mychal made it to the top of the back stairs before Richard stopped her again, "Whatever you said to her made her do this. I do not like your headstrong western woman ways for my sister and I want you to keep them to yourself. She does not need any adverse influences. If the situation arises again, stay out of my family's business."

Walking to her door Mychal replied, "I know I live under your roof, but I will not be told what to do concerning my activities. I am a grown ass woman. Here's an idea, if you tried a little harder, you could keep your family problems from spilling over in to my life. I have enough damn problems of my own!"

It was late Saturday afternoon when Mychal finally woke up and started to move around. She went downstairs long enough to retrieve something to eat in her room. The day went without Mychal seeing Richard all day. She did not even know if Susanna and Tony made it home.

Sunday afternoon as Mychal was on the phone, Susanna knocked and walked in. She saw the suitcase at the end of the bed and frowned, "What is all of this? Are you packing to leave? What happened while I was gone?"

"Okay, I will call you in a little while Ruby. No, I don't think that's possible, but I will let you know. Susanna is here and I want to talk to her. Goodbye." Then she turned to the younger woman who was whispering something in Spanish to the door. "Hello rebel influenced by an American woman. I hope the beach was fun. What can I do for you?"

"It was great! I cannot wait to tell you. I am fine but it is my brother Ricardo who has the problem. I heard he had *berrinche de temperamento adulto*. I understand that he is really sorry about your argument, but he does not know how to apologize for his actions," She winked at Mychal then said louder, "Is that correct Roman?"

He eased into the room, face the color of autumn leaves. Uncomfortable and trying not to look at her, he said in a low, rehearsed tone, "Thanks to my sister, I have seen the error of my ways. Please forgive me and the things I said in my apprehension and temper."

"And . . . " Susanna prompted with a poke.

"And there is no reason to pack a suitcase. You are, in a way, part of this family now and I . . . I sort of . . . want you to stay," he finished looking at the ground.

"Very good. It is a start." Susanna patted him on the back and left saying, *"hacer este derecho."*

Mychal turned back to gathering her things. "I know it took a lot to swallow your pride and huge male ego too, so apology accepted."

"But you are not making any moves to unpack. Why do you still want to leave?"

"Because I can foresee problems with staying here. The things you said in anger is what was really on your mind and heart. You made it clear that being myself will influence your sister to become more like western women. I can't change who I am. My contract does not specify that I stay here in this house. So there is no reason for me to stay where the host thinks being myself, western ways and all, will be a problem."

Richard blinked in surprise and moved within inches of her as if proximity would help his understanding. "No reason to stay? Well I have a couple of ideas that might change your mind. First, I did sincerely apologize. Everyone says things in anger that they cannot take back. If I could, I would take it all back. I know I hurt you with my words, but I hurt myself more by misrepresenting who I am in my efforts with you. I just put us back to day one. In all honesty I think I need you. I am out of date with my family and need you to continue to help Susanna and me, well, communicate."

"Secondly, I cannot deny this growing attraction I have for you. It is you being yourself that I am attracted to. Not seeing you all day Saturday felt . . . off. It is like seeing you every day makes my day better and I am beginning to like that feeling."

He took her face in his hands and gave her a demanding kiss. Without skipping a beat he eased them onto the bed, shoving her bag aside. Mychal broke their kiss by leaving the bed.

"Richard, I will not stay for this weird attraction or because I am a convenient mediator for your family problems. Either you like who I am or you don't."

"Dammit woman! You are making this so hard. Must everything be an argument, a no answer, or a joke?" Richard walked away from the bed and swore in Spanish under his breath. "It does not help that you look like some kind of angry calypso when you are defiant. I have to confess the other night when I held your arm and I thought you were going to attack me, I was both nervous and weirdly turned on. Hell, I do not know how to feel when I am around you. You are not like any woman that I have ever met."

That sounded so cliché, that Mychal had to laugh at his awkward confession.

"So you are laughing at me as well

now?" His long stride brought him back to where she stood beside the bed, "Dr. Ayscue, you are infuriating!"

Mychal laughed harder and mocked, "But I thought you wanted me to stay. Do I need to break your arm so you know how to answer that question?"

Even more crimson than before, Richard told her to shut up, then grabbed and kissed her again. His lips betrayed his demeanor, for they were not angry, but soft and urging. As he pulled her into a body molding embrace, all of her humor was replaced with blossoming desire.

There was a knock at the door, then Susanna called out as she entered, "Mychal, I hope you and my brother made up. I really want you to stay because you are like the best thing that has happened around here. Please tell me you two-" she stopped at the scene in the bedroom, ". . . settled . . . your, um, differences. Yeah, that's a new thing. Okay, well, bye. I will tell you about my trip tomorrow Mychal."

When the door closed, Richard let out a huff of frustration, "Damn! I was not ready for that. I just wanted to feel you next to me. My first time getting you alone all weekend after I acted like an ass and we are interrupted by Susanna of all people."

"Thanks for clearing that up. I did not know if that was a genuine ploy to get me to stay or what."

With a sly lopsided grin, Richard asked, "Did it work? Do you need help undressing, I mean unpacking?"

Mychal put her hands on her hips, "Right now, I don't even know what to say. Just go somewhere so I can think without your distractions."

This time it was Richard's turn to laugh as he left the room.

7

Games and Consequences

After that little weekend incident over Susanna, things inched back to normal for the García-Torres household. Richard did his best to make it up to Mychal. The next weekend they spent a day in the Basque Country. Two weekends later, he cooked her dinner and the family went to light candles in the cathedral. The weekend they were supposed to go horseback riding, Demitri arrived announcing she was on a small holiday. She ruined their plans attempting to monopolized Richard's time. However, she did not ruin Richard's business trip plans the following week.

During that week Mychal actually missed him. At dinner, Demitri was hardly an acceptable substitute. All she talked about was when she and Richard were together. One night, Tony asked her to remind him why they broke up. She gave a short, nonsensical answer, causing Tony to shoot Mychal a sneaky smile.

It was more than dinner conversation that she missed. Mychal missed Richard's companionship. He was fun and that kept her mind off home in the best ways. He did send her texts to let her know he was thinking about her but they were usually late at night when she was asleep. She would get them the next morning which made her sad and smile at the same time. Mychal would text back something cute and playful, only to receive a heart or grinning face emoji.

She was disappointed when he returned so late Sunday night that everyone was in bed. With midterms that week and Demitri monopolizing his free waking hours, they made little time to do more than light conversation and speaking in the morning on the way to work. Mychal was pleased when he dropped by her office one day, during office hours. Richard walked in and closed the door behind him.

"Hello stranger. What are you doing here?"

He perched on some curriculum program sheets she had been reviewing for her next meeting. "Richard, what are you doing? Those are documents for my next meeting that you're sitting on."

"I know, but this is the closest I've gotten to you in weeks," he reached out to caress her face. "I was on campus to see Uncle Juan and thought this would be the only time we might have together for a moment."

Mychal blushed under his touch, "Just until after midterms. Things will go back to normal until finals. I know how you feel.

With everything that has happened these last weeks, I had almost forgotten how you looked, how you felt and the sound of your voice."

Richard leaned over and gave her a blazing kiss. That was not enough for him. He eased off the desk and pulled Mychal into his arms so he could feel her body. The thin cotton shirt as a barrier was almost nonexistent as he could feel her breast harden against his touch. Knowing that this was not the place or time, Richard simply wanted this to last a bit longer. Only in his dreams during his trip to Lisbon, had he touched her. Every night since he returned, he ached to sneak in her room for just one kiss. Every curve felt so perfect to him. The heat from her body excited him. He had to leave before his desire overruled his common sense. He broke their kiss and rested his forehead against hers.

"Mychal, I cannot go on like this. I need your touch so badly. I had to come and see you today. You were all I thought about in Portugal. Making passionate love to you crept into my dreams at night. Feel how much I want you," he placed her hand in his lap.

His growing desire was a welcomed sensation against her palm, "Richard, you know I want you too. But not here in my office, not like this. I want you to know this, me, is what you want. For more than what can happen here in my office and late nights at the house. We will both be cheated if we settle for anything less. We really need to talk about what type of relationship we want."

"You are right." He hugged her. "I know it may sound cliché, but I want our first time to be memorable. We need to work through things to get to that point. Very well then, I will see you at home." With that he gave her a kiss that made her toes curl.

When Demitri suggested that she and Richard, Mychal and her date go out to celebrate the end of midterms, Mychal said a reluctant no. The more She learned about Richard's ex-fiancé turned friend, the less she liked about the woman. She was a spoiled drama queen with a nasty side that she took great pains to hide from others. Mychal said no when the other woman asked, knowing there had to be some ulterior motive. But that was a week ago. A week of the other woman being petty, manipulative, and annoying.

In a week's time, Mychal came up with a plan and an accomplice. She looked forward to the upcoming night with mischievous pleasure. She invited Tony as her date so he could entertain Demitri while she spent time with Richard. She surveyed herself in the mirror, knowing she would be dressed in something the other woman did not own. She wore the most daring dress she owned, a black halter backless mini dress with matching Jimmy Choo sandals. She wore her hair down in chocolate waves with light makeup. Diamond hoop earrings and matching tennis bracelet completed her look for the evening.

She met Richard and Demitri in the library for drinks. Just as they planned, Tony was not there. The reaction she got was beyond satisfying. Richard quietly glowered while Demitri frowned. She wore a slinky form fitting off the shoulders champaign colored dress with stilettos. Richard looked handsome in his dark brown suit and copper colored shirt. He wore no tie, just the shirt buttoned down to the top of his chest hair. Mychal flashed them both a winning candy pink smile knowing neither saw her dress coming.

"Your usual?" Richard asked. When she nodded no, he then asked, "Where is your date?"

As if he had been listening for his cue, Tony entered looking like a typical playboy, saying, "Is everyone ready? I'm starved."

This time Demitri smiled and Richard frowned, face darkening with emotions.

The ride to the city was strained. The limo put them off at Demitri's favorite restaurant; the most chic and reputable in the area. Mychal had never been, but immediately did not like the place because it was too public. All through dinner they were interrupted by people stopping by the table to engage Demitri in conversation. When people were not at the table, Demitri was making Mychal feel like an outsider talking about things that she did with Richard's family in the past. Little did the other woman know that Mychal's attentions were on stroking Richard's leg under the table.

After dinner to everyone's surprise, Demitri directed the driver to stop by the home of a friend who turned out to be hosting a theater party. Mychal and Tony exchanged 'what the hell' looks. Once upstairs at the party, Mychal had mixed feelings among these people. After a few introductions, they split up. Tony went off with some young starlet, while Mychal got a mixed drink and settled in a corner, where she hoped to spend the next few hours being invisible. To her dismay, Demitri and Richard, trailed by another couple found her. Damn.

"Mychal, where have you been? There is someone I want you to meet. Isabella and Emil Jimenez, this is Mychal Ayscue. *Ella es la profesora nueva en la universidad Americana,*" Richard introduced them.

"It's a pleasure to meet you *Señora*. Ayscue," Emil extended his hand. She shook it noticing the manicured fingernails. Mychal thought that this man had the face of a young Hollywood actor, but the body of an old island castaway.

"Dr. Ayscue and it is my pleasure to

meet you both," she shook his hand. The man's eyes took in every inch of her in her tiny dress.

"So you are Mychal. I have heard a great deal about you." Isabella surveyed her from head to toe as well.

"All good I hope," Mychal smiled to keep from laughing at Emil's wife. She was trying to look like the actress Mia Willis at age forty, but looked more like a plastic surgeon's favorite patient who never knew when to call it quits on the quest to look younger.

Isabella returned a fake laugh then, turned to Richard, "Come on darling. You must see Esteban's new masterpiece. He says it is another one to die for."

"I am going to the bar. Anybody want something?" her husband asked.

"My usual," Demitri replied. Mychal shook her head no. "Are you having a good time Mychal? I know it was a short notice. but I just had to stop by and see some old friends."

"As much as I can. I have to confess I have only been to a few theater parties. They're so interesting and full of the acting community acting like they want to be at another party. I never know if people are real or just another character from a previous show," Mychal replied contritely.

"I love them. That is where I first met Richard at the premier party of my fifth play. He was so captivated by my performance and the glamour surrounding the stage. After only a few months, he asked me to marry him." When Mychal said nothing, she went on. "But that was many years and several more proposals ago. Maybe this party will jog his proposal memory. This time I will say yes."

"I thought you said Richard loved you. A man in love doesn't need a memory boost," Mychal spoke without even looking around. "Plus tonight he said that you were great friends."

"Oh yes, friends and more. I am sure Ricardo does not need a reminder of how wonderful a marriage would be, but you know how men are. Even flirtatious ones like Richard can be made into husband material by the right woman; meaning me. All he needed was a little time," Demitri sounded so smug.

"For a man who wants to marry you, how much more time could he possibly need?" Mychal mumbled.

Emil returned with the drinks. He and Demitri engaged in conversation while Mychal gulped her drink and sat mulling over the talk she just had. Richard came over with Isabella and took Mychal out on the terrace to dance. He held her close, listening only to whispers of music.

"What were you and Demitri talking about?" he whispered in her ear.

"Men and time."

"Anything about us?" He kissed the inside of her ear.

"Us? What us? You mean you, me, and your fiancée or just you and her?" Mychal could not keep the bitterness out of her voice.

Richard stopped everything as though he was slapped.

"So you and she have been talking about me. Trading little secrets? She must have said something for you to act this way and say such ridiculous things. What did she say? That I was really going to marry her and keep you as a *concubina* while she was away with the theatre," he was getting embarrassingly loud. A few heads turned in their direction.

"Richard, no it-" He did not even let her finish. He stormed away from the terrace with Mychal in tow via an iron like grip.

"I'm leaving. Now. If you are not

ready or your driver will not take me, then I will call us a cab," Richard hissed at Demitri.

"No, I am ready," she replied nervously.

Tony came up behind Mychal puzzled. "What did you do? *Mi hermano está muy enojado.*"

"I think I went too far."

The ride home was a quiet one. As soon as they got home, Richard was out of the car and in the house with Demitri running after him. Mychal and Tony walked in slowly while she told him what happened. They laughed for a moment and she thanked him for being part of her plans. Then they bade each other *buenos noches.* On her way to her room, Mychal could hear Demitri and Richard arguing behind the closed door down the hall. Oops, she thought then laughed to herself.

Once in her room, Mychal was restless.

She listened to music, wrote letters and checked papers, but nothing would satisfy her need to release her weird nervous energy. When she went out on to the terrace, she spotted the pool. A midnight swim might help. Slipping into a black bikini and grabbing a towel, she headed down to the pool.

Women were like complex math problems to Richard. He just could not understand them. The fight he and Demitri had was one of the worst. She accused him of stringing her along and he insisted their involvement was well in the past. The argument with Demitri ended with him leaving before he inauspiciously threw her out physically. Some things she said were unnecessary and mean spirited. She would not understand there would never be another relationship beyond their current friendship. Their last horrendous breakup was their forever breakup and he was never going back.

And Mychal really pissed him off

tonight. First, she showed up half dressed with his brother as her date. Then she teased him during dinner and finished up the night by accusing him of trying to use her as a mistress. To cool off from both women, Richard headed to the pool. A midnight swim would help clear his head.

Mychal enjoyed the water against her skin in the unusually hot night. Alone, she thought of what she was doing with Richard. Tonight she had played a dangerous game by throwing Demitri in his face. But like everything else in her life over the past three years, Mychal was always on the edge of one adversity or another. Hauling herself to the pool's edge, Mychal was suddenly overcome by despair and tears. Feeling emotionally weary, she fumbled about for the towel. Richard picked it up and handed it to her.

"Thank you," she said before she realized she was not alone. Mychal wiped her eyes to lookup at Richard, whose anger melted at once.

He, in turn, looked puzzled, "Are you crying?"

"Not crying, just chlorine in my eyes. I felt too keyed up to sleep. What brings you out here?" She tried to regain her composure.

"Just needed to cool down and think. I know the feeling," Richard sat down beside her, sounding unfocused and miles away.

Mychal looked innocent and asked, "Are you and Demitri having problems?"

"Oh that is cute. You started everything and act like you did not know this would happen."

"I didn't *start* anything. I just went to dinner with you, your ex-fiancé, and your brother and look what happened," she snapped.

"Is this another joke to you? Tonight you started this date off wrong by wearing the shortest dress I have ever seen and inviting Tony, for whatever reasons. At dinner you started teasing me under the table. Then you provoked Demitri and me into starting an argument. I do not find this funny, nor do I like playing games doctor," he glared.

"Who is playing the game Richard? I admit to the things I did tonight. I took Tony tonight to keep *your* date busy so I could spend some time with *you*. However, when we **started** being more than just friends, I started trusting you. However, you neglected to tell me you were engaged or whatever you have going on with Demitri."

"But I am not engaged," he insisted impatiently, "she and I have been apart for nearly a year. She may still hope for a marriage and tells everyone she sees that is *her* plan. But that is not *my* plan."

"Well, I didn't know any different, even if she does or believes there is a chance for you two. You did both of us wrong." It was Mychal's turn to glare back at him.

"Not so. I admit I should have discussed my past relationship with you when she arrived. I broke it off with her because I did not love her as a husband should love a wife. After the disappointments and pity for so long, I care for her, but do not love her. She strung me along by my feelings. So you see I am the one being, as you said, wronged here." He paused, then said quietly, "I would have told you that when we had our chance to talk, which was supposed to be as we danced on the terrace tonight."

"How the hell was I supposed to know that? All the things she said to me tonight seemed so convincing. It's like she knew to exploit my shaky trust issues. Richard, I'm so sorry," Mychal felt like a jerk. She had inadvertently hurt his feelings and moved to comfort him. Instead he grabbed her wrist and held her at bay.

"I do not need your pity or misguided

sympathy Mychal," he snapped.

"That's not sympathy or pity, that's relief. I'm relieved that you are free and that I wasn't flirting with an almost married man tonight," she tried to explain.

"Really? So, now that it has been established that I am a single man open to do what I want, I intend to finish that cat and mouse game you started tonight." He pulled her roughly to him and punished her mouth with a kiss. Leaving her breathless, he kissed her neck down to wet cleavage left bare by the swim suit. His hand went to her wet bottom.

Mychal stopped him, "Richard, not here. Not out in the open where anybody can walk up on us."

"I am tired of that excuse. I have been through too much tonight and I want you. Now. I cannot make it to the bedroom."

She eyed the pool both comically and skeptically.

"Later, now we need privacy." He pulled her up then led her to the pool house, a single, furnished room. Wordlessly, Mychal laid down on the sofa and invited Richard with open arms.

Instead of going into her arms, he hovered over her and grazed her lips with a kiss. Impatiently, he unsnapped her bikini top. Then hooking his thumbs into the bikini bottom, he peeled the wet material over her hips. Richard took a moment to savor what he uncovered. Smoldering amber eyes, sensual mouth, twin peach peaks, lean abdomen, chocolate triangle and long dancer legs. Richard licked his suddenly dry lips. Feeling overdressed, he discarded his trunks. Without further obstacles, he went into her arms.

Again, he kissed her gently on the lips. Moving to her breast, he took one in his mouth and suckled his peach prize roughly as though he could never get enough of her. His fingers swept down her abdomen past the chocolate triangle gate to her core. He

stroked for a moment then thrust in.
Mychal's whole body shivered. His mouth
and fingers seemed to work in unison to
satisfy her.

She pleaded with Richard to join them
but her pleas only aroused him more. His
mouth moved from her breast to her
midriff. He kissed her navel then moved
down to replace his fingers. He drove her
nearly insane with pleasure. Every stroke
and dip of his tongue sent her deeper into
ecstasy. She cried out his name over and
over.

Finally, Richard knew the time had
come. He shifted his body upward and
eased into her. Mychal let out a long sigh.
Puzzled, he looked down at her. In one
fluid movement she wrapped her legs
around his waist and began a slow pace.
Richard adjusted, meeting each one of her
thrust with one of his own. Gradually, they
became faster and faster, taking them to
higher levels of pleasure. They teetered on
the edge of bliss together.

When Mychal thought she could endure no more, she dug her nails into his back and sailed to the peak of rapture. Her body shuddered as her mind soared. Moments later Richard let out a stream of incomprehensible Spanish and moaned aloud. His breathing labored as his body trembled with pleasure. Both lay motionless. Realizing he must be crushing her, Richard propped up on one elbow transferring his weight. Only then could he see the silent tears streaking down Mychal's face.

"*Mi Corazon, no lures.* Tell me what I did wrong. Did I hurt you?" Alarmed he wiped away the tears with his thumb.

"No, it's not you. I . . .I . . . Richard, after what just happened, we can't go back. I can't. My feelings don't work that way. I just can't go back to the whatever we were before now. This is more than just physical to me," fresh tears rolled down her cheeks.

Richard sat up gathering Mychal in his

arms, his own thoughts paralleling hers. He rocked them and kissed the top of her wet head. He hugged her closer while softly assuring her, "I know, I feel the same way. I believe there is more to us than this moment. Do not cry, everything will be fine, I promise."

8
Holidays and History

Just as Richard said, everything was fine or seemed fine. Demitri left the next morning after their night together. Mychal's days and nights melted by in a delightful yet frightful bliss of time with him. Every day with Richard became more like a dream. But she was leery. The time they spent was wonderful, but she was afraid her world would collapse around her. Every time things appeared to go well, that lull usually preceded disaster.

After the night at the pool house, Mychal's life with Richard changed. He nearly moved into her room. He began taking his lunch with her on days he could leave the office. They had date nights at least twice a week. On Halloween, he, Susanna and Tony gave her some candy and a jack-o-lantern they personally carved. That night, Richard came to bed dressed as a vampire. They had fun undressing each other, making love, then eating her Halloween candy.

Upon his suggestion, they spent time with her closest friends, Ruby and Luis Alcevez. He enjoyed being around them as much as she did. Mychal's favorite time with Richard was winding down at night in bed where they worked, watched TV or just talked about their day. Some mornings they made wild, passionate love before going to work. Richard was everything she had hoped for in someone special. Susanna, Tony, and Ruby were concerned about which direction their involvement was heading.

"Mychal, what is with you and Richard? Is he the reason you float to work every morning? Tell me everything," Ruby inquired at lunch one day.

"What is there to tell? You see everything. Richard is a wonderful man who seems to care about me," she said as she nibbled on her fruit salad.

"Seems darling, that man loves you. When you two came over Friday night, all he and Luis talked about was you. Luis told me Richard has fallen for you." She put her fork down and looked seriously at Mychal, "So where is this relationship going?"

"I honestly don't know. Now, we're somewhere between no longer friends, lovers and commitment."

"And . . . ?'

"And yes, I care for him. And naturally we are growing closer. But we have not talked about anything long term. What good is all this to a relationship that may not have a future? " Mychal questioned.

"You are wrong. Your relationship with Richard does have a future. You need to bring it up and see that you both want the same thing," Ruby replied.

Mychal laughed at the other woman's motherly omens. Furthermore, Richard had too much work to do to give a relationship with her any serious thought.

One Sunday night, Mychal sat on the terrace listening to music. Richard came out and hugged her.

"What are you thinking about?" When she did not answer he tried again, "Are you homesick again? Did something happen with your family?"

She laid her head on his arm and sighed, "You know me so well."

"It bothers you so much. Tell me. Trust me; maybe I can help." He seemed really concerned.

"I didn't leave on the best of terms with

150

my sister and brother-in-law. The fight we
had before I left still haunts me. It's all my
fault, but I really feel like it was his fault
too," she squeezed out a little truth about
her situation.

"No, *Bella*, it is not totally your fault.
Every situation has enough blame to go
around. Call them tomorrow and talk
about whatever it is. Believe me; it will be a
burden off your chest and mine. It hurts
me to see you upset. So call."

"Okay."

"Good, now come to bed and I will give
you a back rub or something like that," he
caressed her breast.

"Do you ever get tired?"

"No, and before it slips my mind; we're
going to dinner Wednesday night," his
hands dipped between her legs.

"With whom?"

"Just us," he kissed her again. "Come on woman before we make love right out here on the chair."

For a while, Richard took her mind away from home. While he slept, she laid awake making mental plans that would work around her secret. If Mychal could not find a way to do that, her future with Richard had the potential to be dead in the water.

Richard's office was at the top of a ten story building. She had only been there a few times and wondered why she had to go get him. They were already late for dinner. Mychal strolled past the reception desk into his office.

"Richard, come on! What on Earth are you doing?" No reply, she walked into his inner office. "Richard?"

"At my conference table. Come in. I will only be a few more minutes."

She followed the dim glow around the corner to his conference table where she halted in surprise. Before her was a table set with candles. A cart stood near with covered dishes and chilled wine. The blinds were open, giving them the backdrop of the city skyline. Beside the table stood Richard, grinning like a school boy with a reward, "Do you like it, *Bella*?"

Tears welled behind her eyes, "Richard, honey, I . . . I don't know what to say."

"Do not say a word. Just sit down while I serve you. I am your waiter and date." Richard ushered her to a chair. To her amazement, he served turkey with stuffing, cranberries, and fresh garden beans. Before eating he made a toast, "Happy Thanksgiving, my love. May we live to see many more."

"Richard, I almost forgot. How did you

know?"

"A good man never tells his secrets. But I knew you would miss your family, so I thought this would cheer you up."

"Thank you so much. But you know Thanksgiving Day isn't until Thursday."

"Yes, I know. But technically it is Thanksgiving in the States now. Tomorrow, you will want to talk all day with your family. So tonight is just for us. Cheers." He raised his glass.

That began one of the most pleasant nights Mychal spent in Spain. The food was excellent and the mood was lighthearted. Richard openly talked about problems at work. She sat and listened, thoroughly enjoying him. She poked fun at what a romantic he was. Together they laughed about their last dinner date. For dessert, Richard fed her various chocolate covered fruits with cream.

After dinner, she sat on the floor

between his legs while he massaged her shoulders. He broke the silence by catching her off guard with a question, "What are your plans for the future?"

"What do you mean, distant or immediate future?"

"I mean distant. Children, career, marriage. Do you even like kids?"

"I love kids. I want a family similar to my own; a big house, white fence and a dog. What about you?" Mychal tried to change the subject.

"One day I will settle down with a wife. We will have children and spend our vacations traveling the world. Just like my parents. What are you going to do when your academic term is up?" he asked in a low voice.

"I don't know," she sighed. "I really like it here. I might inquire about a contract extension or look for another job here. If I go home, things will be different. I might travel some. I'd like to revisit England. I'm thinking about spending some time in Japan studying for my next black belt degree."

"You must really enjoy martial arts."

"Yeah," the conversation was heading into uncomfortable territory. "But I enjoy making you whisper my name much better."

She got up and walked behind his chair. She slid her arms down his chest and began to unbutton his shirt. She nibbled at his earlobe as her hands moved through the thin hair on his chest. Mychal felt Richard shudder beneath her soothing hands.

"Oh Mychal, you do not know what you do to me," he moaned.

Circling the chair, she pulled him to his feet and led him to a moon lit patch on the carpet. To Richard's pleasure, she undressed him shirt only first. She tasted the sweet hollow of his neck, his favorite spot. She caressed and kissed her way down his chest, stopping to suck on the sensitive spots that made his back arch and invoked Spanish mixed with her name. Next, she undid his pants. She glided them over his lean hips. Mychal slid her tongue over the definition of his thigh and calf muscles. Finally, she eased off his boxers. Mychal continued to manipulate his body to the peak of pleasure. Richard thought that he would go insane. He watched as she ever so slowly undid her dress and slithered out. She was not wearing any underclothes. Finally, she straddled him completely naked. Without waiting, he grabbed her hips and pulled her down onto him. When Mychal could not move fast enough to satisfy him, Richard moved his hands on her hips, urging her on. He whispered her name once then lay back on the carpet, drained. Mychal moaned loudly and collapsed on his chest.

For a while they lay there. Mychal was the first to speak, knowing she had to say something on their uncomfortable subject. "I have not given much thought to what I will do. But I know the thought of a long distance relationship is very scary to me."

"Why? We have been growing closer every day," Richard's voice seemed so distant.

"Because, I am not so confident that I am right for you. I am not . . . not the person you think I am." Composing herself, she closed her eyes against her tears and started again, "When I came here, I had a twofold reason. One, I wanted to teach and two, I wanted to see parts of the world that I may never see again. I wanted to travel Richard. I even thought of traveling through the rest of Europe and Asia to research a possible new book. With all that traveling I don't know if I can handle a long distance relationship."

"Do I not have a say in us? What if I can handle a long distance relationship? I have done it before. I can even help you.

Why are you so committed to this line of close minded thinking? You are not even giving me the chance to love you," Richard was almost pleading.

"Richard, I want to . . . I don't want to hurt you because I am uncertain and nervous when it comes to a long distance thing. Like I said, I am not the person you think I am. Richard, I have never had a long distance relationship. That's why I am not so sure it is right for me or for us. You say you can do a long distance relationship and I believe you could with someone like Demitri. You cannot with someone weak and unsure like me." He tried to rebut, but she cut him off. "Listen these are just my thoughts right now. Again I am committed to you but am not sure how the long distance thing would work with not knowing where I will be after my contract is over."

"But you do not know what the future holds and you are not giving us a chance." Richard was growing upset.

"Just thoughts Fueled by the uncertainty of strange territory for me. Don't get upset."

"No more talk about your thoughts. I really want to enjoy the rest of our night," he kissed her forehead and gave her a lopsided grin. "While I appreciate christening my office, I think it is time to go home."

Mychal and Richard were quiet as mice as they eased into the house and tipped down the hall way headed for the back stairs. They were so careful to be quiet, neither noticed the lights on in Richard's study.

"Richard! Darling, come in here," Demitri called from behind his desk.

Holding hands, Mychal and Richard walked into what looked like a mess. Demitri sat at his desk with papers scattered everywhere.

"Demitri, what are you doing here?"

"Well, I thought this year we would start early on planning the Christmas party, so I flew in early."

He sighed, "Demitri, I have been so busy at work because of my upcoming trip to Cuba, that I do not have time to coordinate the yearly festivities. I was going to hire someone this year."

"No need," she chirped, "I will do it and make sure it is done right. Were you working late tonight?"

"No, I treated Mychal to a holiday dinner. Listen, you might as well call it a night because I have no plans of getting into anything beyond sleep at this point. We all had a long night and it is getting late. *Buenos noches*." Richard headed toward the door with Mychal wondering what would happen next. She shot the other woman a 'really you went there' face.

"But darling, I hoped you would have a night cap with me," Demitri whined.

"Goodnight Demitri," he called, pulling Mychal up the stairs behind him.

Once in the room, Richard headed for the bathroom and Mychal sat on the bed to undress. She called to him, "Hon, you were a little cold with Demitri tonight."

"She ignored you."

"Yeah, but that doesn't justify your attitude," Mychal frowned.

"Listen, after our last discussion I did not expect her to still be acting this way, like nothing happened. If she does not understand it is over when I tell her, maybe she will understand my actions." Richard stood in the doorway, wearing only boxers brushing his teeth. His wide shoulders tapering down to a slim waist and muscular thighs reminded Mychal of the superhero build of every comic book character.

"Have you told her about us?"

"No, because who I am with now is none of her concern. I have made it perfectly clear there is no future for she and I beyond an indebted friendship. Period. Besides, she is not stupid. I did not come upstairs with her and I am in your room." He headed back to the bathroom. "Do not worry. If she cannot accept or respect that we are a couple now, then that is her problem. How about we forget her little intrusion and enjoy each other for the next four days? Cuba will be terribly lonely without you."

Even after a relaxing bath, Mychal could not get her mind off the things that happened tonight. Her thoughts were on the future, she and Richard discussed earlier. She complained about him not being straight with Demitri and she was lying to him the whole time. She liked to think of it as sharing selected information and reserving other knowledge for another time. All things considered, not telling him everything was the same as lying. The lame excuse of not being able to handle a long distance relationship was the worst cop-out she could have come up with. She made up her mind to tell him the truth after the holidays. Maybe by then, something would work itself out at home.

Richard was right, Thursday was spent video chatting with family. Mychal enjoyed her brothers, nieces and nephews, but dreaded talking to her mother and especially her sister. Never failing to disappoint, the holiday was not complete without a pity party of one jealous sister. In bed that night, he listened to her fume about her stupid brother-in-law and simple sister, their mother's favorite child. He teased her saying that she sounded like a teenager. For that she hit him with a pillow. Their pillow fight turned into a playful wrestling match that she let him win as they were both turned on within minutes. In the end, both pillows and clothes were discarded in the pursuit to please each other.

Their weekend was spent blissfully lounging by the pool during the day, dancing at the local hot spots in the evening and leisurely making love at night. Nothing mattered to them outside of their time together. Monday morning came all too quick. That morning, she helped him pack. He was playful and clingy, wanting to hold her every second. It was as if their Thanksgiving conversation had him thinking he was never going to see her again. At the door, while they waited for Pedro to bring the Alpina around, Richard embraced her again. "I will think on the future of our relationship while I am gone. Mychal, please, do the same. I want to love you. Give us a chance."

"You have my word I will." With a final kiss, he was gone.

Mychal went upstairs and cried as she got dressed for work, feeling like she temporarily lost her best friend. If him leaving for a one week business trip set off her waterworks, a long distance relationship was looking more like it would no longer be an option. She would stay in Spain. Great. The simpler things got the more complicated they became.

The next two weeks were filled with preparations for the annual Christmas party and decorations for the house. For Mychal, those weeks were filled with finals. Her mind was busy so she had no time for Christmas spirit or shopping. She could not wait for the end of the semester and her vacation to begin. Since coming home from his trip, she and Richard saw each other at night when they wearily went to bed until morning when they went their separate ways for work. His trip to Cuba produced a new client in a new client market.

On the first Monday of Mychal's holiday vacation, she and Susanna went Christmas shopping. Along the *Gran Vía,* she bought a painting for one brother and silk sheets for her other brother. For her sister, she bought a watch and had it inscribed. Her last purchase for the afternoon was an antique locket for her mother. The last two gifts she had sent by special overnight delivery. Satisfied with the day, the two women went to an early dinner.

"What did you get for Richard?" Susanna asked between forking salad in her mouth.

"Nothing yet. Have any suggestions?"

"I think you should marry him for Christmas." Susanna teased.

"Not funny," Mychal rolled her eyes. "Get serious. I haven't gotten anything for Richard, Tony, or Demitri. I owe Tony something extra for being my wingman when I needed him. I mean for Demitri, I would like to give her a clue. But I also want to honor whatever customs you have for giving gifts to family friends. Would it be petty to give her a suitcase as a hint to leave us alone? "

"Funny. But that means you have already gotten mine," Susanna grinned. "Look, get Demitri some earrings and Tony wants things that appeal to women. That was easy. You have to get Richard something special."

"Something that appeals to women? Like what?"

"Will you forget Tony for the moment? Richard is who we are talking about. Maybe something that the two of you can share, exotic romantic, and exclusively for two," the younger woman babbled on.

"Like a trip," Mychal said quietly to herself.

"Exactly!" Susanna grinned slyly.

"Wait, neither one of us has time for a trip. Where would we go?" Mychal quipped.

"A romantic little island like the Mallorca . . . hmmm . . . maybe even one of the Virgin Islands," Richard's sister suggested.

"No," Mychal interjected quickly, "they are so close to home that I have been there many times before."

The younger woman shot her a puzzled look. "What about Paris?"

"I know the place to go, but it will take a few days to arrange a trip like that. Anyway, what's our next stop?" she absently asked.

"A small boutique I know. Maybe I will find a gift for Demitri." Susanna signaled for the check.

"Does she normally come around for the holidays? I mean if she and Richard have been broken up, why would she spend her holidays with his family not hers?"

Susanna shrugged, "When they were dating she would occasionally stop in for events and on various holidays. I hated those times because they would always have some argument or drama. When they broke up, we had about six months of peace. Then they, meaning she, decided that they could at least be friends, so she had a reason to stop by overnight when working in the area. Richard would stay at work late and come home to sleep in one of the guest rooms or his office because she was always lying in wait in his room. She told Tony that she is actually staying the entire holiday."

"Wonderful," Mychal shot out.

"I know. The thought of her around for Christmas, just gives me a warm feeling in the pit of my stomach," the younger woman teased.

"Me too."

The rest of the evening Mychal spent absentmindedly shopping. Besides buying Demitri a brooch and Tony's hoodie and matching workout pants, she bought toys for her nieces and nephews. As soon as she got home, Mychal wrapped all her gifts. She put all her family's gifts in one box to be shipped to New York in the morning. She would ask Richard to send them through his office.

It took a few days to make all the trip arrangements. All the activities going on in the house, kept Mychal busy. She had no time to get the tickets. With Christmas Eve just four days away, she went with Richard into the city to finish her business. She dropped him off at his office building then went directly to the travel agency. Pocketing the travel arrangements and cottage reservation, Mychal walked to the nearest shop. By the time she left, it was time to pick up Richard and head home.

After storing the box from her family in the back seat of the Range Rover, he got in and kissed her.

"Everything all closed up for the holidays?" she asked.

"Yes, now we can spend more time together on our first Christmas," he grinned.

"Richard, I am not sure of your traditions, but can we exchange our gifts on Christmas Eve?"

"Why?"

"Well, what I got you is something you might not want your ex-fiancée to see," she blushed.

"Oh, I see. *Bella*, I am really disappointed that you still let Demitri get to you. I thought we talked about this. You said her being here this holiday was fine with you."

"Does it matter? In any case, it's not like you can kick her out." Mychal chose her words carefully before adding, "I know you have not come right out and said the words 'I am with Mychal now'. That is unless you did it and didn't tell me."

"No, I did not do either. Why are we having this conversation again? I have said all she needs to hear on this matter. I am not with her and who I am with, is none of her concern. She wanted to assume the duties of the Christmas celebration and I let her out of nostalgia for my family. But I would have said something to her earlier if I had known letting her do the preparations upset you all this much."

"She doesn't upset me! It's just that she. . . aw, hell, she is beyond annoying as hell. She's been doing the Christmas preparations like the grand diva of the manor or something. She hasn't had much to say to me, but I know she probably hates me. Especially watching you live in my room while she sleeps alone in the room the two of you used to share. If I were in her shoes, I would feel the same way,"

Mychal's voice softened.

Richard let out a long sigh and massaged his temples. "Mychal, you are too kind to sympathize with her. And believe it or not, I understand a lot of what she is going through. But I am not the cold hearted uncaring ex-fiancé. Since you want to be sympathetic, look at this from my point of view. I stopped seeing Demitri sometime after the holidays, this past January. After wasting six years of my life and countless hurt behind rejected proposals, we ended on a terrible note. She threw an adult tantrum that lasted for a few days. Demitri screamed and destroyed things. She wrecked my other truck. She tried to have me taken into custody for assaulting her after blaming the bruises on me, not the accident. After her volatile outburst, she should be glad that I continue to speak with her, let alone allow her to stay in my home."

"I continued to associate with her because I feel indebted to her. She was there when my parents died and I will always feel obligated to her for that reason only. We will always have some type of camaraderie because everything was not terrible in our relationship. But when I asked for my ring back, that was my closure to our relationship and should have spoken volumes to her about any chances of a future relationship. I did not even date, because I did not want to hurt anyone when I knew I was not ready for a new relationship."

"So six months later, after living like a combination of a recluse and a monk, a totally unpredictable coincidence, positioned someone new into my life. Unplanned, seemly uncontrollable events happened that drew me and this new person together. So now as my new happiness grows, almost a year later Demitri decides she wants to pick up where we left off like the whole break up never happened. If my desire to have more than that one sided waste of time she and I called a relationship makes me a cold hearted bastard, then that is what I will be." His voice began to rise, "For once in a long time, I deserve what I believe to be a chance with someone who can fulfill my life. I will not permit her to ruin it for me. We *will* exchange gifts on Christmas day with the rest of the family. End of discussion!"

They rode a little while in silence, with him looking out the window and her looking at the road, each in their own little world. Richard was wrapped up in how to handle the upcoming holiday. He really understood Mychal's point of view, but he was upset. She simply did not understand *his* viewpoint. Demitri was not going to be allowed to ruin his first holiday with the person he loved.

Mychal was not privy to the emotional maelstrom that Demitri put him through for six years. The first year, she put him off for her career. Then, his parents passed away within months of each other. He needed time to heal and she urged him to do so. It seemed the more he pressed her to talk about marriage, the more she pushed him away. When he got tired of pressuring her, she had a change of heart and wanted to get engaged. That was four years ago.

Four years of her being his part time fiancé and him being her full time arm candy. Every play opening, every television performance, every popular magazine had their picture in the social pages. Almost a year ago, he could not make it to a social event due to work issues. Demitri threw a fit that lasted for days and ended in him asking for his ring back a month later. Ever since, he had been licking his wounds and ignoring her manipulative attempts to worm her way back into his good graces.

Mychal was always under the impression until her recent conversation with Susanna that things were wonderful in Richard and Demitri's relationship. She thought their breakup resolution was a friendship. She was quite floored at the

177

information that Richard shared, but glad
at the same time to hear there was never a
chance of him ever getting back with
Demitri. While she wanted to secretly
rejoice, this new information coupled with
the constant awareness of her own situation
made things difficult. Counting to ten,
Mychal broke the silence. "Point taken. I
feel I owe you an apology. I didn't mean
for my insecurities to start an argument."

"I am just tired of you always hating
what she does but then appearing to defend
her actions. Honestly, I understand why
she is here this holiday and clearly see her
motives. Mychal, she is trying to come
between us. I will not let that happen and
neither should you!"

"I know. It won't happen again," she
promised, feeling worse.

"Good. I wanted us to exchange gifts
on Christmas so everyone could see what I
got you."

"Give me a hint," she pleaded, trying to lighten the mood.

"No chance."

When they arrived home, Richard took Mychal's box from home upstairs, then went to see about the decorations. Once alone, she began unpacking the box. Taking out Styrofoam peanuts by the handfuls, she reached her first gift. Her brother, Max, and his wife sent a new party dress. This one was gold and would fall just above her knee. Sexy and short, just the way she liked them. Under that were pajamas from her younger brother, Reece, and his family. Next, was a new red swimsuit with cut outs from her sister, Riley. Mychal had her sister buy Susanna's gift and wrap it in pretty snowman paper. Finally, she got to her mother's gift; a silver frame with a picture of everybody back home. She blinked back the tears in her eyes. Under that gift at the bottom of the box, there were Christmas cards and letters from everyone. The ones from her nieces and nephews made her laugh, but the serious ones really got to her. Her sister wrote how sorry she was about the whole mess but she was torn between her sister and her husband. Everyone missed her. By the time she finished reading, the tears streamed down her face. What a mess of deceit and emotions her life had become!

She absently packed things up and wandered to the garden. The December night was only chilly against Mychal's thick Carolina Hurricanes sweatshirt. To Mychal it resembled a frosty October night back home in New York. On the stone bench she cried and thought of Richard. She had not come here to fall in love with him. She came here to put a little space between herself and the possibility of an investigation into Jacob's dumpster fire of a business back home. After her year was over, she had planned to continue living abroad for a while. She had known the first night she and Richard made love, there was no turning back. She was determined to find a way out of her mess. Somehow, she would find a way for their happiness. This whole situation made her sick. Standing up to leave, Mychal felt dizzy. Taking a few seconds to gain control, she made a beeline for her room. A cold splash of water helped put everything back into focus. She emerged minutes later in a cold sweat. She changed into a tank top and boy shorts and got into bed. Minutes later Richard came in.

"Mychal, where are you? You went by in such a hurry I did not-" He saw her in the bed, "What is the matter *Bella*? You are all pale and sweaty."

"Something I ate did not agree with my tummy," she attempted a smile.

"But you have not eaten dinner. I will call Luis."

"No. No, really I will be fine. I just need some rest and I'll be fine in the morning. Okay?"

"No dinner?"

"No, just crackers or something. And a little club soda. But maybe later."

"All right. But if you need anything, call." He kissed her forehead.

"Thanks. I think I just need to rest."

"Richard," she called him as he turned to leave, "I believe we have a future. It won't be easy, but we have one."

He smiled, "We always did. Am I to believe it took you feeling sick to figure that out? Was that your stomach's way of telling your head and your heart?"

"Oh shut up and get out," she pulled the covers over her head.

9

Parties and Lies

Mychal stood in a familiar place; in front of her bed with dresses everywhere. It did not take long to narrow down the choices. Her fourth party dress was not right for the occasion, so that left three. The black dress had a head piece she could not find and the jade dress was surprisingly too tight. That left the white gown she had bought for a masquerade ball two years ago and the electric blue dress that she wore to a neighbor's wedding last year. Mychal frowned because both looked a bit much for the occasion. Donning a robe, she went to get Susanna. The younger woman complained as she was unceremoniously dragged to Mychal's room.

"Really Mychal, what's wrong that you cannot pick out your own dress? I have my own dress dilemma but you don't see me dragging you to my room. I know you are sick, but does that impair your judgment?"

"If you just say which one is appropriate for tonight, then I will let you go."

"Okay," Susanna looked at the dresses, "The white one is beautiful, but those big sleeves are dreadful. The blue one is more in season. Wear it."

"Thank you. Now you can go."

After a quick shower, she sat at the vanity applying makeup when Richard came in. "*Bella*, fix my cuff links please."

Mychal loved him in black tie. His tux was tailored accenting his V-shaped athletic frame. She noticed the initials engraved on the onyx between the diamonds were not

Richard's. She gave him a warming smile, "Nice hon, I think your father would approve."

"Yes, I think so too," he held out his arms. *"Bella,* do you feel up to this? I will understand if you want to stay in. Hell, I want to stay in bed with you too."

"We already talked about this. I'm fine. Are you almost dressed? As you can see, I'm not," she tried to throw a hint.

"I need my shoes and jacket. I wish Demitri would stay in another room. I would open the other wing if I thought she would stay over there. Of all the other bedrooms in this house, why does she insist on occupying mine?" he frowned.

"Wishful thinking on her part. Now come get me when you're dressed," she shooed him out.

Again, she sat at the vanity. She curled her hair into soft waves that framed her face. Next, she disrobed and stepped into the strapless gown. The dress accented her waist and showed cleavage that was just enough to be elegant and alluring. The full skirt had a thigh high split showing off Mychal's legs and French pedicure in strappy silver heels. She contemplated her appearance in the mirror, thinking how much her look would definitely upset Richard's ex. Lastly, she dabbed on perfume and with Swarovski crystal choker in hand went to find Richard.

"Oops!" she exclaimed as she bumped into him outside the door.

"I was just coming to get you." She turned so he could zip her up.

"You are so gorgeous. I cannot leave you tonight for one minute." Richard put on her necklace then kissed her neck while rubbing himself against her bottom.

"You behave. You are too sexy in black tie," Mychal complimented him, smiling at the anticipation of his ex's reaction.

"Honey, could we please not grand stand tonight? You are a wonderful host who knows how to throw and work a party. I love to watch you work the room; it's kind of hot. But I do not wish to be a part of the hosting show as that spotlight is all yours. Please, no grand entrances, formal announcements, or speeches."

"Why? I want the world to know that I am crazy about you. What better place than among a hundred or so of my friends and family?" He gave her a pretend sad face.

"Because," she hugged him close, "I want you all to myself, just outside of the spotlight."

"Later tonight, believe me," Richard winked.

"Please, Richard. I'm not one hundred percent and don't want to call more attention to myself. Please?"

Looking into her pleading amber eyes,

he sighed in reluctant agreement.

Silently, they took the backstairs. But as Mychal feared, as soon as they reached the party, people gathered around them. Richard was by her side or close by all night.

The *Noche Buena*, Christmas Eve dinner was like nothing Mychal had ever experience. The seafood dishes were exceptional. She had something called *besugo* and another native dish *lombarda* made with cabbage. Throughout the evening he introduced her to countless people coming in and out of the party. Some kissed and hugged her after introductions, while others eyed her suspiciously. She did see Rafael, who came over to say hello. They passed a few words of congeniality before he moved on. The only person Mychal really knew was Morcheeba, Richard's secretary and cousin. Glad for a friendly face, she talked with her the longest before finally managing to break away to chat with Susanna.

"Mychal, you look fabulous. I cannot even tell you are sick at all. That dress looks great on you. I did a great job with the selection."

"You did, thanks. This party is huge. Do you know all these people?"

"I know most of the relatives and friends, but business associates, not really. Demitri made up half the guest list. Speaking of her, did you see the look on her face when you two made an entrance? Pure hatred. I had to laugh," Susanna chuckled.

"Well, serves her right. She is the one who wanted to plan her ex boyfriend's family Christmas party knowing he is involved with someone new. She's someone who needs my foot in her-"

"Mychal!" Ruby called. The older woman wearing a festive holiday colored dress came over to hug her, "Dearheart, you are so beautiful tonight. That blue is your color. Susanna, there is a boy in my French literature class looking for you. I saw him in the living room last. Be a dear and go find him so he knows I told the truth about relaying the message."

"That would be *Señora* Diamontopolos' son, Enrique. Mychal, he is cute," She wet her lips before walking off toward the living room.

"So Ruby, are you having a good time?" Mychal asked.

"It is much better now that I have seen you. Never mind that. You and Richard look great together. I hate to say it, but I told you."

"Please not tonight. No love lectures. No motherly fortunetelling episodes. You can resume all that when the semester starts." Mychal rolled her eyes.

"And I most certainly will when the semester starts. Look dearheart, I have a gift for you. Do not let me forget."

"Ruby, you really didn't have to."

"Nonsense. Who is that woman coming over here? She looks familiar. Is that the ex-girlfriend that has been giving you all the trouble? She does not look too happy."

"Nobody," Mychal murmured really not in the mood for the ousted ex-fiancé slash party planner. Damn, was she ever going to leave them alone?

"Well, do not let her ruin this evening for you and Richard. If you need me I will be close by."

No sooner had Ruby turned away did Demitri start in on Mychal, "I did not know you were well enough to come down to the party."

"It was not my idea, but I'm here," came the dry retort.

The other woman was elegant in a one shoulder red jeweled gown. Mychal had to give her kudos because her hair and makeup were flawless, adding to the overall presence of the Greek stage beauty. "You may think that tight blue dress and feigning illness can charm Richard, but I know better. Do not get in my way. I am a woman who gets what she wants and I want Richard."

"Oh cute, a threat. Is the feeling mutual?"

"Evidently, or else he would not have come back to his own bedroom last night," Demitri replied smugly.

"Well, you are staying in his room. The man has to get clothes every day."

"Which clothes are you referring to, the ones in the closet or the ones I removed last night?" The other woman's smile was icy.

Mychal, feeling a twinge of queasiness, was done. If Demitri wanted that game tonight, she was ready to play. "What are you really trying to say? That Richard spent the night with you? You need a reality check because you are trying too hard. I know what he was doing last night because he came to bed and told me, like he does every night and morning when we wake up together in our bed. What will it take for you to leave us alone? He. Has. Moved. On. But right now, I'm done with you and your lies. So if you will not go away, then I will leave you alone. That way you can get use to being by yourself, because Richard is with me now. You know as in a couple and the sooner you get that reality check, the better off you will be."

With that Mychal stormed her way through the crowd.

As the night wore on, Mychal's feet began to hurt. She was worn out from the eating, dancing, cheering, and having countless discussions about America. She slipped into the family room where the Christmas tree lit the room. She sat on the rug with her dress fanned out and took her shoes off. Alone, at last, she relaxed.

"There you are. I have been looking for you," Richard knelt in front of her. The Christmas lights gave Mychal a dim glow. "Why are you sitting in the dark? Is something wrong?"

"I'm tired and I didn't want to pull you away from your guests."

He took her hands in his and kissed her forehead. "I know I have to do the hosting thing, but I am tired too. Just countdown Christmas with me and then go upstairs."

"Can we do it alone in here?"

"You know better than that. We have to be with the family for the countdown. Come on Mychal, please." His green eyes, bright with anticipation, pleaded to her as well.

"All right, pull me up." Hand in hand, they walked back to the party.

". . . Five, . . . four, . . . three, . . . two, . . . one! *Feliz Navidad*" The crowd cheered and applauded for Christmas as confetti fell from the ceiling.

Richard took Mychal in his arms and tenderly kissed her. Then he looked into her glowing amber eyes and said, "*Feliz Navidad, Bella.* I love you."

Tears gathered in her eyes and she whispered, "Oh Richard, Merry Christmas my love."

Once in her room she shed her clothes and replaced them with a robe, while Richard stayed downstairs seeing that the guests left and the extra help was paid. Her thoughts were racing as she paced the floor anxiously. Richard said he loved her and she replied like a reflex. If he loved and trusted her as he said, she would have to tell him the truth. But how? Mychal put on her favorite music and sat on the sofa to think about the ways this situation could possibly go.

When Richard walked in, that is what he saw; Mychal on the sofa staring into space. A deep scold marred her face. "Mychal?"

She jumped at the sound of her name, "You scared me."

"What were you thinking so hard about?"

"Did you mean it when you said you loved me?" she questioned.

"Yes."

"Then I have something to tell you." She led him into the bedroom. "Sit down."

"What is this about?" Richard began to get uneasy.

Mychal got her make up case and sat on the bed. She took out everything including the fake bottom. While attending to this task, she spoke without looking up at him, "I have not been totally honest with you about myself. I . . . you know I wrote a book. Well, with the royalties from the book I made some investments with my brother-in-law. They all turned out very well. That's how I could afford these."

She took out a few black cases and opened them to show various gemstones in earrings, pendants, and bracelets, different cultured pearls and a couple of diamond necklaces. She removed deeds and titles. "This is some of what I own. I put most of my stock in a trust for my nieces and nephews before I left. I kept my cabin in North Carolina and beach house in New Jersey. I'm telling you this because I don't want you to love someone who is not honest with you. I know I should have told you before. But it wasn't until tonight, when you said you loved me, that I knew I could completely open up. I finally let go of my trust issues and want to commit to loving you completely in this relationship."

"We lay beside each other every night sharing everything and you could not trust me before tonight?"

"That's not what I meant!" Mychal
took a breath and started again, "People are
judgmental. Just like you were when I
walked in this house. Now tell me and be
honest. What would you have thought if I,
a stranger on a college professor's salary,
came here looking like an actress at a red
carpet event? You would have thought
something was wrong with that picture.
You already thought I somehow
manipulated the situation to get here with
my name and made that known on day
one. When things finally settled down and
we made a conscious effort to be on better
terms, I did not want anything to mess that
up. Plus my financial status back home or
how I got it, seemed inconsequential to
your obvious lifestyle. Besides, I really
didn't know if things would change
between us if I told you that I was not your
average college professor."

She paused, "Wait, there is more.
Before I left there was a huge family fight

198

about this very matter. I abruptly left the business arrangement with my brother-in-law due to his less than above board business practices. My sister was beyond furious because she said I didn't believe in her husband. She took the whole business abandonment and distancing myself from her jerk husband personally. She took sides and it was not mine. I came here feeling like I abandoned my own family in a time of crisis and used yours to cope. It does not look like it, but I kind of feel like I partially influenced this whole current situation to make me feel better about my drama back home. Your family was what I needed to fill a void. Then you and I turned into us with me feeling torn between wanting the wonderful relationship you offered but not deserving it. So I am not this wonderful person you think I am," Mychal lowered her eyes in shame and rubbed her temples. "Has anything changed? If you love me, does it matter? Will you please say something? Anything?"

"You did not let me. What you just told me was a little surprising, but nothing has changed. I am sorry the business dealings with your family did not work out. I could see from day one that something beyond moving here was bothering you. I hate it was a fight right before you had to leave for a year. But hopefully it will work itself out. Family can be a tough call, look at what you walked into with me and Susanna. If anybody is guilty of influencing a situation, then I am too. I used you to repair things with my sister. You filled that void that she and I needed at the time. That being said, you are not some evil cunning mastermind that has done so many terrible things that you do not deserve someone to love you." Richard loosened his bowtie. "As far as the other things, I am proud of your accomplishments and you. Your work paid off and you enjoyed success. That is not something to be ashamed of or to hide. And yes, I still love you

"Not disappointed?"

Richard cupped her face and smiled. "Disappointed, why?"

"Because I didn't tell you sooner."

"Mychal, trust is something that is earned. I understand how you felt because people, myself included, are disparaging. And although we are in this relationship now, honestly things were rocky at first. I am sure that fact added to your inner emotional turmoil. You and I are only humans doing the best we can at any given moment." He hugged her close as his hands wandered inside her robe. "And at this moment, I want you."

"Richard, all this stuff on the bed."

"Oh yeah. Put it away while I shower."

Mychal put her items back in safe keeping. Richard dressed in a towel brought her a wrapped gift.

"I thought you wanted to wait until Christmas day with the family."

"I still do. Ruby gave it to us," he explained.

Mychal laughed and tore at the paper, "I forgot. Earlier she was giving me relationship omens."

Inside the tissue paper was a silver framed photo of her and Richard, Luis and Ruby. The bottom of the frame was inscribed 'Friends Forever.'

"That's sweet." Mychal smiled then frowned when Richard took the frame from her, "Honey, what are you doing?"

"Making sure I have your attention," he said as he embraced her. Making quick work of her robe and his towel, Richard rolled on his back pulling Mychal on top of him. He kissed her with all the urgency of an anxious high school boy. He took his time tasting her curves. Each time he gently sucked or kissed a supersensitive spot, Mychal drew a sharp breath. His hands caressed her bottom, molding her to his evident manhood. Swiftly Richard rolled over and joined them. He set a pace that exhausted and fulfilled them. Afterward, Richard slept soundly but Mychal stayed awake. She contemplated the choice she just made. As Mychal drifted off to sleep, she was at peace with the decision of telling him enough of the truth to convince herself she was no longer lying to the man she loved.

Christmas with Richard's family was much like the holidays with her own. After breakfast everyone sat around the tree unwrapping gifts. Susanna squealed when she opened the short, low cut black party dress from Mychal. Richard just shook his head.

"This is your gift from Mychal," Susanna handed the red gift bag to Richard.

He fished through the tissue paper and produced orange swim trunks, "Thanks

Bella, but you should have said something if you did not like my other trunks."

"No, you clown," Susanna joked.

Richard looked again and blushed, this time producing two airline tickets and a mini braided rope. "Mychal, these are round trip tickets to Phuket, Thailand. Really, a holiday in Thailand sounds wonderful, but a bit much."

"Yes, it does," Demitri dryly interjected before taking a sip of wine.

"Neither of us has the time for a vacation. And what about the other arrangements?"

"Richard, all the arrangements have been made. Our cottage is booked. We are going on my spring break in March. It gives you enough time to get your work affairs in order. During our time there, we are going zip lining through the forest," she finished with an impish grin.

Richard opened his mouth to say something else and Mychal cut him off almost whispering, "I just wanted to share one of my dreams with you. We don't have too many forest zip lines in New York."

Everyone in the room seemed to hold their breath waiting for his response. Susanna broke the awkward silence with, "Now, where is hers?"

Richard relaxed and blushed as he handed her a small square box. Mychal opened it to see a smaller black box. She ashen a little and said a silent prayer; hoping it was not an engagement ring. She flipped the top to see a large emerald cut sapphire, flanked by two diamonds set in a gold band. She turned to Richard, mouth dry. "Richard . . . I . . . I can't accept this. This is really too much. Please, I don't know what to say. No, I can't take this," she shoved the box in his hand.

"Of course you can. It is not an engagement ring. Think of it more as what you Americans call a promise ring. I saw it and thought it would look perfect on your finger. The color is perfect." He took it out of the box and slipped it on her right ring finger. He squeezed her hand as she tried to pull away. "See, I told you. If you love me, you'll wear it. You will wear my promise. Besides no ring, no Thailand."

The room was swallowed in an uncomfortable pause. Even Demitri looked back and forth between the two. Feeling defeated by his romanticism, she kissed him and said, "I do love you and I will wear your hopelessly romantic sentimental promise. Thank you honey."

Tony spoke up to break the moment, "Now that is settled, we need to get ready for more relatives."

The García-Torres family knew how to celebrate Christmas. People started arriving for *Día de Navidad*, the traditional Christmas lunch. After lunch, there was music and folk dancing in the grand room.

Richard's Uncle Rico sang beautifully as Susanna accompanied on guitar along with her cousins. Richard hugged Mychal from behind and swayed them to the music. After that fun affair, the projector came on in the grand room so the men could watch soccer games and tell stories leaving the women to make more food for the evening meals. Mychal really liked Richard's relatives. They all made an effort to speak English to her. She talked with the older women in her broken conversational Spanish. A couple of Richard's aunts asked when the wedding would happen and his great aunt was the most avid. With Morcheeba interpreting, she asked Mychal all about their relationship; insisting that they would be married soon. Not knowing what Richard told his aunts, she just smiled and played along.

Demitri, now openly despising Mychal, rarely acknowledged her presence. She still mingled with Richard's family during the day. A few times Mychal caught her scowling in her direction. Instead of making a scene at a family function, she just ignored the other woman. Richard and his family seemed so happy, that Mychal was not going to let anything in her power ruin the day. Hopefully after the events of the holiday, the other woman would leave and never come back.

As the festivities wore into the night, Mychal went to her bedroom to call home. To her dismay her brother-in-law was arrested for government fraud the week before Christmas and implicated Mychal as his partner. Some investigation officials called her mother on Christmas Eve with some questions. Mychal assured her mother that everything would be fine. Her older brother was an attorney and had instructions on what to do in case of this emergency. It took time to calm her mother down. After wishing her a Merry Christmas, she hesitantly disconnected the video chat. She took a deep breath and went downstairs, hoping she looked happier than she felt.

After a erratic night's sleep, Mychal got up feeling miserable. She thought things would have gotten better, with Jake getting arrested but bonded out. He was trying to make her lose everything, which now included Richard. At that thought, she burst into tears. She cried so hard she made herself sick. The rest of the day she spent moping. Every morning after that, Mychal got up miserable and crying. A worried Richard called Luis Alcevez.

"Luis, she cries every morning. The day after Christmas, she made herself sick. She barely eats. I know she misses home, but I do not think this is normal."

"Is she sulking around all day? You know, moody and depressed," Luis inquired.

"Yes."

"I think this might be more than a simple case of homesickness. She needs to get out and do something to shake this depression. I have an idea. You and Mychal should go out with Ruby and me on New Year's Eve for *Noche Vieja*. We will go do something that Mychal likes to do. It will get her out of the house and give me a chance to talk to her."

"Great," Richard agreed.

"Meet over at my place around seven. Nothing fancy mind you, just jeans and a coat for an evening on the town."

"Thank you Luis. See you then."

"Anytime, my friend," the doctor hung up.

Richard did not say anything to Mychal until the morning of New Year's Eve. He intentionally spoke curtly. "I know you're homesick, but this thing is eating you alive. We are going out tonight. I am telling you now so you can pull yourself together before this evening. You can be mad at me for making plans without consulting you, but I did it because I love you."

After he strolled out the room, Mychal's eyes welled with fresh tears. When she emerged from the bathroom after an extra hot shower, Mychal's attitude had changed. Her somber mood was replaced with anger. How dare Richard talk to her like that, make plans without her consent, then order her around? She went to find him to tell him a piece of her mind, but he was gone. All day she stalked around. When Richard returned late that afternoon, Mychal jumped on him ready to fight.

"Where have you been? You marched in here this morning and ordered me around. Then you disappeared all day. Who in the hell do you think you are? I am not a child and I warn you not to treat me as such," she glared at him.

"Mychal, I love you and just hate to see you depressed. Ruby and Luis suggested we go out and I agreed. We all just want to see you smiling again. You know, take your mind away from what is happening at home for a while."

Mychal's anger dissolved. He was just trying to help in his usual clumsy, romantic way. Her eyes clouded over.

"Please, do not cry again. Come on upstairs while I change clothes."

From the time they met Luis and Ruby, Mychal enjoyed herself. Everyone dressed and acted like teenagers. They started out at *Puerta del Sol*, went from party to party throughout the night. Their last stop was a dinner club. Luis had reservations for a late dinner. Richard danced with Ruby so Luis could talk to Mychal.

"Is anything wrong?" Luis inquired.

"No. Why do you ask?"

"Well," he watched her closely for reactions, "Richard says you've been depressed lately. Sometimes crying yourself sick."

"Luis, he makes it sound worse than it is. This is my first holiday season away from my family. I'm just not coping well. But soon the semester will start and work will occupy my time," she patted his hand.

"All the same, I think we should not keep delaying the follow up from your physical. You have an appointment coming up in a few weeks."

"Luis, I will not have time. You know classes start in the next two weeks. That will be the busiest time for me," Mychal protested.

"No excuses," he replied sternly, "I am now your doctor and I know what is best. My nurse will call you with an earlier appointment time when we have a cancellation."

"Please don't tell Richard. I don't want him to think something is wrong. He is already on edge and worried about me and my family back home."

"All right Mychal. But you're making me choose between professionalism and a concerned friend."

Mychal covered his hand and said, "You don't have to feel torn. When he asks, you say that you talked with me and you will keep these things in mind for my physical. That's all true. Just don't tell him we are trying to move my appointment up."

"You are not lecturing Mychal, are you sweetie?" Ruby hugged her husband.

"Lecture, no. Little counseling, yes."

"Does this mean she's not going to cry anymore?" Richard asked.

"Yes it does," Mychal yawned.

"Tired *Bella*?" he teased.

"Just a little. You know I'm normally in bed by now," she joked, winking at him.

"Must you two be so obvious?" Ruby

giggled.

"¡*Díos mío!* woman. Can't you see they are in love?" Luis sighed.

The two couples rang in the new year with more dancing and eating grapes at the countdown. Later in the early morning hours after dropping the older couple off and returning home, Richard sat massaging Mychal's back. She pondered how to approach the subject of her attitude lately then said, "Thank you for taking me out tonight. I had a good time."

"I knew you would. I just hated to see you depressed," he kneaded her shoulders.

"The holidays made me more homesick than I thought," Mychal sighed. "Things are not much better between the family and me. I think Christmas made things worse."

"You will not have to worry about that in a few months."

"Yes I will. I'm not planning to go

home."

Richard was glad she could not see the relief on his face. "Where will you go?"

"I don't know yet. If I get a job, I will stay here. Or move someplace that the distance will allow us to continue our relationship."

"You have been doing some serious thinking. I get it now. So do you like it here that much to call it home for a while? Or is it me, your all-knowing, all caring host with the most?" he teased, pleased to hear her say that.

"Well, you all are the closest family I have, besides my own. And then there's us. I love you and want you in my life, even if I live in another country. I can't let what we have go, due to distance. I love you enough to work on the long distance relationship if it comes to that."

"I love and need you. I will not let it come to that," he hugged her.

Mychal sighed heavily and sagged in his embrace. The weight of the situation back home seemed to physically bare down on her. She believed Richard would do whatever he could to make them work. If only he knew what a relief and burden what he said was at the same time.

10
Secrets and More

Mychal was never so happy to see the semester start. She attacked her classes with vigorous energy. She joined two more university committees. She spent her time away from classes exercising. Every morning she ran and a few nights a week she worked out in the garden.

The afternoon of her appointment with Luis, Demitri stopped by. Mychal sat grading assignments when she blew into her office overdressed and statuesque as usual, "Mychal, how are you?"

Mychal looked up from the computer

screen and removed her blue glasses. "I'm fine but confused. What are you doing here? What can I do for you today?"

"I came to take you to lunch."

"Well that's, er, nice," she frowned, "but I have an appointment in less than an hour."

"But I insist. I feel like Christmas was an awkward affair. Maybe if we just chatted with no outside factors, we could find common grounds to get along. I would like that very much."

Alarm bells went off in Mychal's head like she was in a New York City fire station. This was clearly some kind of setup. But maybe it would be their last. If she could somehow make the other woman realize her pursuit of a relationship beyond a friendship with Richard was pointless, maybe she would finally leave them alone. "If you just insist, we can go to a place a couple of blocks away."

Demitri smiled, "As long as it is my treat. I know professors do not make the same salary as theatre personnel."

That was Mychal's confirmation red flag. She mentally acknowledged it and packed up her laptop to leave for the day, knowing after this meeting and the appointment, she would need to go home.

Once seated in the café in a quiet booth, they ordered drinks and salads. Demitri had been pleasant on the walk there, talking about her new show and its press release. Mychal still did not trust her and soon grew tired of the facade.

"So Mychal, how has school been?"

"Demitri, you didn't ask me out to discuss my work. Why don't you save us both a lot of time and get to the point?"

Her smile dropped immediately, "Fine, I want you to leave Richard alone."

Mychal sighed, "Okay, we have been

through this before. You persist. You start with me, then you go to him. You two fight. You leave. You come back and try again. Same cycle, same result. You know what people say about the definition of insanity."

"I am not insane and you are not what you appear to be," the other woman shot her a smug smile.

"Meaning?"

"That you, sister-in-law of Jacob Adams, are a criminal. I stopped in New York City while in the States. It did not take long for me to find out what kind of legal trouble you were in. Your brother-in-law has already been arrested. According to the papers, you and he were in his criminal business together. However, you just happened to be out of the country." Demitri shook her head in mock pity, "All that profit the two of you made with the government's money. Who bought that house your mother lives in? You? I stopped by for a visit, but no one was home. It is such a shame that-"

The sound of breaking glass halted Demitri and some people in the cafe. The glass Mychal once drank from was now shards in her hand. Ignoring her bleeding hand, she braced both legs against the table in the booth and shoved it toward a startled Demitri. The woman had no time to react and was pinned in the chair between the wall and the table. Mychal was on the other woman with lightning fast speed. She stopped less than eight inches from her face and spoke to Demitri with open contempt and hard amber eyes. Her tone was all hate and deadly business, "Listen to me carefully, because I will not say this again. I don't care what you know about my private life back home. Your threats are hollow to me. But you crossed the line when you tried to visit my mother's home. What is between me and you has nothing to do with my family. If you ever, ever go near or think of going near my mother again that would be the worst mistake of your sad life. If I get a call that my mother thought someone was following her, a stranger was outside the house, or somebody rang the wrong doorbell only God can save you from me. You will spend the rest of your life depending on a straw for most of your daily living. I hope my message is loud and clear! Do you understand?"

Demitri just looked at Mychal, too shocked to respond.

Mychal grabbed her laptop bag then snatched a towel from a passing waiter on her way out to wrap her bleeding hand. "Lunch is on her tab."

Without stopping, she walked across campus to the medical center. When she walked in, the nurse jumped up to attend to her cut hand. Now, with her lab work done and her wound cleaned up and closed with a couple of stitches, she sat on the examining table waiting for Luis. He walked in with an exasperated expression on his normally jolly face.

"What happened to you? Your blood pressure is sky high and you had glass in a cut in your palm."

"I tried to hit Demitri with a glass."

"Mychal," he looked in her ears, "sometimes I wonder why you waste your time with that woman."

"She asked me to lunch."

"You could have said no. You know better than to engage her," he checked her lymph nodes. "What did she say?"

"She warned me to stay away from Richard. She wants me to leave him. She's so . . . so . . . damn aggravating."

"And over presumptuous. Breathe. Again."

"That thing's cold," Mychal complained.

"Quiet! Breathe again and let it out slow," he listened for a while. "Lie back please. What did you say to her?"

"I didn't say anything. Much. I left before I hit her. I did kick her with a table."

"Mmmmm," he felt her abdomen, listened with the stethoscope and tested her reflexes. "Okay dear, put your shirt on and come to my office. I need to confirm some things."

Slowly she dressed, then walked in his office. Luis sat behind his desk on the phone. He motioned her to take a seat.

He hung up and walked around to sit on the corner of his desk. "Well dear, from the looks of things you are pregnant. Some gland swelling, hardened uterus and elevated temperature. I called to confirm by your urine sample. What can I say? Congratulations? You and Richard are going to be parents."

"Oh no. Oh no. No, no, no. Luis, this

cannot happen. My gynecologist at home said I have a tilted uterus and have been on the pill for so long there was a chance of infertility. You said I could not get pregnant at least a year after I stopped the pill! Hell, I am still taking it now. I mean like, if I forget one day I double up like I'm supposed to on the next day. Today I was coming in to talk with you about starting another contraceptive other than the pill. I mean we used condoms and over the counter stuff. Kinda, I mean most of the time."

"In normal situations that is correct. The body adjusts to different situations, meaning physical changes, medication side effects, dietary shifts, and even different climates. If you have been on the same pill for more than ten years it was probably time for a different, stronger dose when you moved here. We discussed dietary adjustments and medications at your last appointment, but had no idea then how active you would be. Also, not taking the pill correctly does not really help, does it?"

"But Luis, I would have known. My sister-in-law was sick every day. She missed periods. She gained weight. Where were my signs? I still have a light cycle," Mychal tried to rationalize.

"Mychal, everybody's pregnancy is different. You have gained a little weight. You were not supposed to have changes in your cycle because of the pill. Sometimes women who exercise skip morning sickness. But some do not. You are not acting very happy about this."

She sighed, "I don't know if I am."

"Richard will be happy. He is always talking about kids in his future."

"No." She jumped up, "Not a word to anybody."

"Okay," he agreed, "but in a couple of months or so, everybody will know. Your body will change even more. Your breasts will produce milk and your weight will start to show more."

"So, what now Luis?"

"Now you see a local obstetrician, preferably in the next two weeks or so. The sooner the better. If you want, my nurse will find one and make an appointment. We need to pinpoint a due date. My advice is to increase your water intake and watch your weight. You are healthy but a bit underweight for nearing the end of your first trimester. Eight to ten weeks, if I had to guess"

"Ten weeks, really?" a shocked Mychal hugged him, "Not a word Luis. Not even to your wife. I will tell her. You're the best."

"You take care and congratulations, I think."

Mychal left his office in a daze. She walked straight to Ruby's office where she burst into tears. "Mychal, what on earth is wrong?"

At that question she cried harder. After some calls Ruby came back to her. "Now, we have all afternoon. Start talking and I mean from the beginning."

Mychal started at the beginning as requested. She explained how her brother-in-law got a small business loan from the government under pretense. She and he were going into business with that loan and the royalties from her book. Instead he invested all the money in the stock market on an insider tip. They made a fortune. Later, he told her the non-profit business was just a shell company. She demanded her return share and dissolved the partnership. He still kept the business front and occasionally used her name. An investigation was beginning when she left, resulting in Jake being arrested before Christmas. Now, Demitri knew everything and threatened to tell Richard. In addition to everything else, she just found out that she was pregnant.

"Mychal, I do not know what to say. This time I do not have any advice. Your situations both here and at home are quite unusual. What did my husband say?" Ruby frowned.

Mychal's bottom lip trembled.

"No, wait. I do know the best advice. Tell Richard. He will understand. But, tell him now," Ruby sighed. "Come on. I will take you home."

Since Mychal rode to the university with Richard, Ruby drove her home while she texted him that she was going out and would meet him at home. Only Susanna was there when they arrived. Although she was calmer when the younger girl asked her troubles, tears ran from Mychal's eyes. It was Ruby who told the other woman about Mychal's situation.

"Why did you keep this from Richard," Susanna demanded.

"When I came here, I had no intentions

of getting involved with him. I told him some of the stuff happening back home. Besides, I thought the problem would get fixed during the year I was here."

"Well, it did not. What were your plans after your contract was over?"

"I was going to apply for a permanent position here in the area. If not, I was going to London, or somewhere close so we could still have a relationship. I have even thought about getting an apartment and teaching online. We just talked about this over the holidays. About how we could make us work even with a long distance relationship."

"And now that things have changed, what are you planning? A marriage to my brother Richard would be so . . . so beneficial," she smirked.

"Susanna, I don't know what you're implying, but you're wrong. Whatever happened between now and then has not changed the way I feel about Richard. I do love him. Maybe marriage was in our future, but not this way. Not because I'm pregnant." Mychal was puzzled by Susanna's reaction.

Also puzzled by his sister's reaction, Ruby intervened, "Susanna, I do not understand why you would accuse her of planning this pregnancy so Richard would marry her. I was under the impression your brother loved her enough to consider marriage anyway. You know her better than me and I know Mychal did not do this on purpose. I was also shocked when she told me. But I think the other side of the coin is more important; a woman is in trouble, pregnant and scared."

"Scared?"

"Yes, scared," Mychal's eyes watered again. "Scared to tell Richard and scared to be pregnant. Not too long ago, I was on medication for nausea, some cold medicine, I still took my birth control pills, and drank when we went out. I didn't know. Now I don't know how it will affect my unborn child."

"I did not think about that," the younger woman's voice softened. "I am sorry Mychal. I just knew you had somehow planned this. What did the doctor say? What will Richard say?"

"Nothing and don't tell him. I will tell him soon enough. At this point, I don't have a choice."

"You need to tell him before Demitri does. That woman will use this information to drive a wedge between the two of you. He needs to hear the whole story from you to keep him from getting the same ideas as Susanna. Are you going to be all right?" Ruby kissed her cheek. "I'm going to pick up Luis. If you need anything just call."

"I will leave you to your thoughts. I'm just right down the hall."

Both women left Mychal to her misery.

Richard could tell something was bothering Mychal. She was jumpy and moody all week. Then there were the stitches in her hand. When asked she said she cut her hand on glass at a restaurant at lunch. Luis had a nurse clean the wound and put a couple of stitches in her hand. She dismissed the whole thing as the glass was probably cheap and her being clumsy. He believed her until she threw in that last part. He knew she was anything but clumsy. Before it went any further, Richard asked her the problem, "Mychal, is everything okay?"

She quit brushing her hair and thought for a moment. "In a sense; yes. I'm having worse trouble at home. Do you remember when I told you about my sister choosing her husband over me? Now I am public enemy number one. Things will never be the same between my sister and me. I think it will be a long time before I go home again."

"Why did you not say something to me?"

"Because, I'd like to work it out myself. You know if there was something you could have done, I would have asked. This . . . this thing with Riley and Jake is a living nightmare."

"If there is anything . . ." he trailed off, his dark green eyes registered concern.

"I know honey. But I need you to make me a promise. Whatever happens to me and my family, you will still love me. No matter how bad things get or take a turn for the worst, promise me that I will still have your love and support. Promise." She twirled the ring he gave her for Christmas on her finger.

Richard came and sat in front of her. "Of course. Nothing is so terrible that I will stop loving you. Please, tell me what it is because you are scaring me."

She kissed him gently on the lips, "One

day soon. Just remember your word."

The day arrived when the once postponed Demitri swept in one night on an unannounced visit, catching everyone off guard. Susanna and Mychal were in the library researching music therapy when Tony ushered her in. She did not even call ahead which meant she wanted to surprise everyone, especially Mychal. Richard came from his study, his mind already made up to stop his ex-fiancé's intrusions once and for all.

Knowing how she would feel, Richard requested, "Mychal, *Bella* could you go check my laptop? I think I left it on."

"No, stay. I think she knows why I am here. Have you told Richard yet? You know I gave you enough time." The other woman eyed Mychal suspiciously, looking for signs of movement. The incident at the restaurant let her know the doctor could move with amazing agility and speed.

"Tell me what? Is there something I need to know?" He looked from one woman to the other, utterly confused.

"I see she did not heed my warning. Yes my darling Richard. You need to know that our dear professor is a white collar criminal. She is wanted for government fraud back in the States. It would appear that she and her brother-in-law set up a business to get money from the government. He invested the money and they made a fortune. Except," she turned, still wearing her coat to smirk at Mychal, "he got caught and she got away. This little trip was convenient, just what she needed."

Mychal did not say a thing. It took everything she had not to look at Richard. The silence in the room was terrible.

Demitri continued, "So you see Richard, this was just what she needed for a clean disappearing act. This job, this trip and you. I even have proof." She produced a New York paper with Jacob's story in a small section on the back page. She made a move to hand the paper to Richard but the dark look on his face changed her mind.

Mychal was still silent, not trusting her own voice.

"Mychal, say something. Anything," Susanna pleaded. "If you will not defend yourself, at least tell him the rest. No more secrets."

This time she did look at Richard and said quietly, "I did not mean for it to happen but I am pregnant."

"Pregnant?" Tony echoed.

"Pregnant! *Skatá*! Whore! I should have known you would plan this; just like you planned everything else. Trying to have a bastard child so Richard would marry you and you could stay in this country." The other woman looked at her figure. "It looks as though it is still early. I am sure Richard can find a place for you to handle this . . . this unfortunate problem."

With practice explosive speed, Mychal was out of her chair and the back of her hand swept across Demitri's chin with staggering force. The sound echoed across the room like a cannon startling everyone as the other woman stumbled backward. Mychal's cold, hostile voice followed, "Enough! Don't you even say that! I have stood here and listened to you accuse me of what you think you know. But I will not stand here while you talk of my unborn child as a pawn, to be used or destroyed. This is my child."

"Demitri, if you ever come near my child or cross me again, I promised you before a miserable life, but I'm telling you now that you will not live long enough to regret it." She turned and walked out the room. She did not make it halfway up the stairs before she burst into tears.

Susanna looked at Richard with hard dark eyes that were relentless. "You did not even want to hear her side. You did not even stop Demitri from bullying and belittling her. She has been through so much. She needs you right now more than ever. Papa would be so disappointed, he did not raise us this way. I hope you are happy."

She turned to Demitri who was just regaining her composure, "I hope you are pleased with yourself. But I do not think you realize that what you just did, changes nothing. He still will not run back to you. You are nothing to us."

Susanna spat at the woman's feet before leaving the room.

Moments later Tony looked at them both saying nothing, but eyes conveying astonished disappointment. He opened his mouth to say something but sighed and shook his head. Still wordless he followed his twin sister. He found her and Mychal talking.

"If you leave it will not accomplish a thing," Susanna argued.

"What is there to accomplish?" Mychal almost shouted. "Thanks to Demitri, I did not get a chance to tell him anything on my terms. Now everybody thinks I'm some kind of criminal mastermind that snuck out of America in the dark of night. Jacob Adams is arrested while Mychal Ayscue is a fugitive from justice. All she was missing was the victim in the situation, my poor baby sister Riley. Hell, she made it sound like the whole damn thing was my idea."

"I did not believe her," Tony spoke up from the doorway. Both women stared at him. "Doc, even in the short time you have been here, I know you are not that kind of person. From what you just said, I know you did not do those things she accused you of doing."

"Thanks Tony. Now will you please drive me to Ruby's? I will be staying there a while."

"Yeah. These your bags?"

"He certainly will not. You need to stay here and talk to Richard!" Susanna exclaimed.

"No, I think he . . . no wait, both of them need some time apart. *Hermana*, cooler heads need to prevail in this situation. Come on Doc," Tony picked up her bags.

She hugged Susanna, "I will be in touch later. Bye. We will get together on campus."

11
Hurt and Alone

After that night, Mychal set about planning her next steps in her immediate and coming future. She did research on London, figuring it would be more like America. She decided she would make two trips: one to job hunt and one to make living arrangements once she had a job. Mychal also began to job hunt in the immediate and surrounding areas. She invested considerable time in learning what online universities had brick and mortar campuses in the surrounding areas as well.

She packed up the personal things in her office and had the custodian move the boxes to the graduate assistants' office. In short order, she moved in with Ruby and Luis, to make sure she did not see Richard. It took Mychal a few weeks to get her belongings from the house. Whenever trips to the house were necessary, she went in the daytime when no one was home. She tried to avoid Richard as much as possible. She would not return his calls. If she saw him coming to visit her office, she would immediately leave. She needed some space to figure out her next move. She loved him and knew just one talk would cloud her judgement. To keep track of her, Richard resorted to calling Ruby and Luis.

With more urging from Luis and Ruby, Mychal began to look at homes to rent if she stayed in the area. She made a list and was going over each location with Ruby the night Richard paid an unexpected visit.

"Richard!" Luis quickly recovered and called for help, "Ruby, dearheart, Richard is here!"

Ruby was sitting with Mychal on the computer in the sunroom. She ordered Mychal to stay put and left. Mychal eased closer to the door to hear the conversation and catch a glance of Richard.

"Where is she, Ruby? Where's Mychal?" Richard seemed unsteady on his feet. His clothes were wrinkled and he had a six o'clock shadow. He looked like a disheveled mess.

"She is not here. Richard, have you been drinking?" Ruby eyed him suspiciously.

"Did you drive here?" Luis asked more concerned.

Richard stood up a little straighter attempting to regain his dignity, "I drove here to find the woman carrying my unborn child. Did she leave you too? You know she left me?"

"Richard," Ruby warned, hoping Mychal would stay put as ordered. Though she was short, Ruby moved her body to block his view of the house.

"Well, that is what happened. She took my child and my heart and she left. I love her." Richard's voice broke, "I wanted . . . I wanted to marry her. I had planned to ask her in February on America's Valentine's Day, but she won't even answer my texts! Every time I go to her office, she is gone. She comes to the house when nobody is home. She is avoiding me! It is like she wants nothing more to do with me."

"I know you wanted to marry her, *hijo*," Luis sympathetically patted him on the back, "I know you want a family."

"Richard, why didn't you tell Mychal you wanted to marry her that night everything was coming out? She knows you love her. Everybody knows you love her. But that night, you should have supported her, or defended her, or something. Anything. If you knew how Mychal felt about that woman, why did you even continue your friendship with her?"

Defeated Richard's shoulders sagged, "I don't know. Demitri knew I loved Mychal. My ex understood that she and I would only ever be friends. I should have known something was wrong when that woman showed up unannounced. I even tried to avoid them being in the same room. That moment was insane. Everything happened so fast. So fast. Accusations were flying. It was confusing. Then Mychal told us she was pregnant and my ex suggested that she get rid of the baby. Out of nowhere, Mychal slapped Demitri and left the house. Like I said, it all happened so fast."

"But-" Luis tried to speak, but Richard continued, his words slightly slurring, "When I finally calmed down, I listened to what Demitri had to say then asked her to leave. Leave my home and my life and never come back. I really should have done that when we became official. I guess I thought Demitri could handle just being friends. Knowing her past, I misjudged the situation. This whole thing with her involvement could have been avoided."

Richard took a shaky breath, "Then, I thought about all the times Mychal kept trying to tell me she was not who I thought she was. All the times she wanted to talk, but just sighed or cried. At Christmas, she showed me all this stuff and told me how she got it. She told me all about her family argument regarding bad business partnerships before she left. I let her know then I supported whatever she was going through. I was also just proud of her accomplishments and did not see past that. She was trying to reach out to me but things kept getting in the way. Luis, I know Mychal would have told me everything eventually. When she was ready. Would that have affected our relationship? No, because I love her. Now she is avoiding me. She will not see me or take my calls."

Ruby said, "Dearheart, maybe she is still not ready. Maybe there is more to the situation than you know. Maybe she is hurting behind it, just like you."

Richard sighed heavily. Tears spilled down his cheeks, "But I made her a promise. I gave her my word that nothing she could say or do would make me stop loving her. I just want to talk to her. Just want to see her. Just want to hold her. I just need her Luis."

"And she needs time," Luis felt sorry for him. "Let me take you home. Tomorrow is another day. Maybe she will come to her senses and talk to you soon."

Ruby followed Luis to take Richard home while Mychal cried herself to sleep, missing Richard and utterly miserable.

Ruby had two evening classes so it was a few days before she got around to discussing the incident with Mychal. As soon as dinner was over, she started in on the younger woman. "How many times have I said 'why don't you just talk to him'? Then he shows up on our doorstep drunk and raving about how much he loves you, and you still would not talk to him."

"You told me to stay put," Mychal was trying to avoid the conversation.

"I did not know exactly what Richard wanted. Once I saw and heard how pitiful he was, I got him to say the things he has been wanting to say to you for weeks. Still, you did nothing," Ruby punctuated every word in the last sentence.

"I wasn't ready. Anyway, I am considering moving to London again if that is the Richard that I will have to deal with."

"You are being unreasonable!" exclaimed Ruby. "You are running away from the problem. Again. Now you are talking about carrying this child to another country."

"Just think about this. You do not

know anybody in London. Who will help you care for this child?" Luis came in on the end of the conversation. "Have you even seen the obstetrician I suggested?"

"Luis with all that has been going on, honestly no. How is London any different from here? I didn't know anybody at first here either. Now I know you. London is closer to home. My brother can fly in and help me some times."

Luis shook his head, "Mychal, you are making a bad situation much worse. You need to talk to Richard."

"I can't. He is a good man who deserves a life without my drama." Mychal could not keep the tears from sliding down her cheeks.

The older woman put an arm around her. "Mychal, life is not without drama, as you say. My husband and I have been married twenty seven years and have three children. There was always some drama.

But therein lies the strength of your relationship. Relationships that work weather the storms, obstacles or whatever. Relationships that are weak just crumple and fold like paper. Just look at that Greek girl he was with. As soon as he laid eyes on you, her chances with him were a memory. Besides, do you think his happiness would have come from a relationship with her?"

"I can't say," Mychal answered weakly.

"Liar, you can too. This man was in your bedroom every night. He shared the pain of his last relationship. He accepted that your relationship might be a long distance one. He gave you a ring for Christmas. You two were going to Thailand. Mychal, you are talking nonsense. I will support you if moving is your decision, but I will not like it." Ruby turned to her husband, "Luis, I will hear no more of this *despropósito*."

"Mychal just stay until the baby is born. I do not suggest moving to another country during pregnancy. Anything could happen. The change of water and climate might have an effect on the pregnancy. The stress of the move could trigger a miscarriage, even in the second and third trimester." Luis softened his tone a little, "Dearheart, you have to stop thinking like a scared fugitive and start thinking like a parent-to-be. I know you have done most things by yourself and are comfortable with that fact. I know you are afraid to accept help from others, but you need people! You need Ruby and me. You need Richard and his family."

"Think about this scenario: you are on your way to work and you are in an accident. It takes all day for the authorities to identify who you are because you are unconscious. Meanwhile, your nanny is concerned because you have not come to pick up your child. As evening turns into night, the nanny knows something is wrong. She is calling your emergency numbers locally, but these people are in the hospital with you trying to contact your family in America to find out the nanny's name to get the baby. Your brother calls the nanny to tell her he cannot get a flight until tomorrow night. Your nanny is frantic because your brother will not be there until the next night and your friends cannot take the baby for different reasons. Your nanny works another job on the weekend. She is stuck between a rock and a hard place and thinking about leaving your child with one of her relatives that you do not know just so she can go to work. When your brother gets to London no one will know where your child is in a super large and foreign city."

"That's extreme Luis," Mychal frowned.

Luis gave her a piercing look with hard blue eyes, "Extreme, but possible. That is why I believe moving to London is really turning a bad situation into a worse one. You might as well move back home, have the baby where your family can help, then face your punishment or consequences for your legal predicament. That way, you still have a network to help raise your child. You may miss the first five years or more of your child's life, but your child will have a loving support system to grow up. One without his or her father though. London is not an option. The smart choice is home or here. Madrid is large enough that you could live here and not see Richard. You would have Ruby and I to help and possibly Tony and Susanna. Does that make sense?"

After a deep sigh, Mychal replied, "Yes it does, but-"

"But all I am asking you to do is think about it," Luis interrupted.

"I was going to say that I would think about it. You didn't let me finish." Mychal huffed.

"Really Mychal, what Luis is saying makes sense. Either go home or stay here.

Whichever one you pick, you will have to deal with Richard. He is the child's father. He does not strike me as someone who will shirk his responsibility. As a matter of fact, he might even want custody rights, once the baby is here. But you will never find out what he really wants to do if you do not talk to him. Please, just talk to him once," Ruby pleaded.

"No. Maybe. Hell, I don't know."

"You cannot avoid him forever. You will have to make some arrangements at some time. Besides, if he did not care, he would not have driven over here drunk the other night to cry in my foyer. Mychal, I am trying to be a supportive friend, however I cannot do so without being honest. This idea of moving is irrational and unsafe to the baby and you are not being fair to the man you say you love." Ruby emphasized the last part.

Across town, Richard lay in their bed
reading, which was doing him no good.
Another sleepless night. Richard had not
had a full night's sleep since Mychal left
nearly a month ago. Finally in frustration,
he threw the book down and turned off the
light. He laid in complete silence. A breeze
came through the partially opened terrace
doors. The breeze seemingly brought the
smell of her hair. He closed his eyes only to
see her hazy amber eyes staring back at
him. Richard shook his head trying to clear
it. The medicine he took for his cold was
having a worse effect than he thought.

When he opened his eyes again, her
scent was gone. He turned over and could
have sworn he saw her, but only for a
second or two. Then, he realized it was
only the sunrise announcing a new day.
Another realization hit him like a splash of
cold water; he was alone. The only woman
he had totally given himself to was gone.

After a cold shower to start the morning, Richard unwillingly proceeded to work. He still had a fever and chills, but he refused to stay home. Most of his morning was spent coughing and wondering how Mychal and his unborn child were doing. His dazed trance was interrupted by his secretary, his cousin Morcheeba, buzzing in. *"Ricardo, las autoridades están aquí.*

Puzzled, Richard replied, *"Sí.* Send them in and hold my calls."

Two officers entered the room. A small woman in plain clothes accompanied by a uniformed taller man. Richard shook their hands, "I am Roman Garçia-Torrés. Officers, is something wrong? What can I do for you today?"

The male officer spoke first, "Officer Pharr. Thank you for your time today. *Señor,* do you know Demitri Salvos and

Mychal Ayscue?"

"Yes, *Señora* Salvos is or was a family friend and Dr. Ayscue is my . . . she is the mother of my unborn child," saying that was painful to Richard. He unconsciously winced.

"Are you okay?" the officer asked.

"*Sí*, thank you for asking. Just dealing with a really bad cold right now."

The small Filipino woman spoke, "Detective Baird, *señor*. Were you aware of two incidents involving these women about a month ago? One at Nico's restaurant on the campus of the American College of Madrid and I believe the other incident was at your home."

Richard was too sick to be pretentious. Suddenly he felt overwhelmed and tired. He let out a heavy sigh, "Yes I was there when Mychal, I mean, Dr. Ayscue slapped *Señora* Salvos. *Señora* Salvos threatened our unborn child and Dr. Ayscue got a little emotional like pregnant women can get. Next thing I knew she smacked the other woman and left."

The officers exchanged looks. Detective Baird spoke first, "So you are saying that *Señora* Salvos threaten *Señora* Ayscue first?"

Richard watched the other officer taking notes on a notebook that magically appeared. "Yes, Demitri said something about killing our unborn child."

"Were there other witnesses?"

"Yes, my sister and brother were there as well? Detectives with all due respect, I have answered all of your questions. How about an explanation behind this little inquiry?"

The slim woman nodded, "Fair enough. We are here investigating allegations of assault and attempted murder."

"Of?" Richard waited, half scared to hear the answer.

"Demitri Salvos."

Richard gave them an incredulous look, "It sounds like you said Demitri Salvos. When?"

"Once at the restaurant and once at your home."

Richard dropped his head, letting out a chuckle.

"Is there something funny *señor*? I know you said that you were ill, but you are acting a little strange as well."

"Come," he motioned them to his conference table, "sit down and I will tell you want happened so you can write it all down."

For the next half hour Richard told the pair about that night. He also told them about how Demitri had once falsely accused him of attacking her when they broke up and that was a matter of court records. He went on to discuss how she

had destroyed his truck when they broke
up over a year ago. He continued by
saying he had no idea what happened at
the restaurant, but he was sure if they did
more digging, they would find, Demitri
had somehow provoked that too. He sadly
remarked she was a very good actress and a
master at lying to audiences for money.
Richard finished by saying she was an ex-
girlfriend that had not taken their break up
well. Their transition to being family
friends was contentious to say the least.
She would not give him a moment's peace
even in his new relationship with the
mother of his unborn child.

The room was uncomfortably silent
after his story. When Detective Baird
spoke, her tone softened, "*Señor* García
Torres we had no idea. I am truly sorry for
all that you and your family have been
through. If you will give your siblings
information to my partner, we will cross
check witnesses' statements and present
our findings to our captain. We do need to

locate Dr. Ayscue though. At some point, we will need her statement as well."

"She is on a small holiday. If you give me your cards, I will share them with her when she gets back." Richard lied with a weak smile. He took their cards and gave them Tony and Susanna's cell phone numbers. He ushered them out, bidding them farewell.

As soon as he sat in his chair, Morcheeba buzzed again, *"Hay dos hombres la consulta americanos está en la línea cuatro."*

Mystified, Richard replied, *"Sí.* Transfer them and take messages for my other calls."

The Americans wanted help following up on a case of government fraud in New York. A possible person of interest was a professor they were told may be working at the American College of Madrid. As Richard held the main benefactor position of rector of the board of visitors at the university and was involved with the outreach programs, they were wondering would he know of a professor named Mychal Ayscue.

Richard pretended to think then said, "I think I recall seeing Mr. Ayscue's curriculum vitae at one of the meetings."

"No sir, *Dr.* Ayscue is a woman," the man on the other end of the phone sounded impatient.

"A woman doctor named Mychal Ayscue? The board voted to hire for that position, but I am not sure of the person. I can have the board of visitors' secretary check and get back with you."

"No, no sir. We'll take your word for it. This was just an inquiry on a possible lead. But if you hear anything concerning where this Dr. Ayscue may have taken a position in Europe, please give the embassy in Madrid a call." The other man spoke in a soprano voice.

"Certainly, you have the university's full cooperation on this matter. Good day gentlemen," Richard was never so glad to end a phone conversation. He immediately picked up the phone to contact Mychal. She was not in her office. He tried Luis and Ruby's but nobody was home. He then tried her cell, knowing she would not answer. He left messages for Luis and Ruby. Feeling more miserable than ever, Richard cleared the day and went home to get some rest.

Mychal was expecting an envelope from her mother so she had to go by the house to pick up mail. She let herself in and made a beeline through the house for the mail on the kitchen counter.

"What are you doing here?" The sound of Richard's voice made her jump and mail scattered everywhere.

"I came to get my mail. I thought you would be at work," she attempted to collect some of the scattered letters.

"I am not feeling well," he bent down to pick up the rest for her.

"You don't look well. You should go to bed."

"And you look, well . . . pregnant. But healthy." He noticed her larger chest straining against her shirt when she bent down and her hips seemed fuller when she stood up.

"Thanks. Well, see you." Mychal turned, determined to leave before she burst into tears. She had not been this close to Richard since she left. Just seeing him made her chest ache.

As she turned to leave, Richard's mind debated whether to let her go or try to keep her there. Aware of the consequences, Richard cleared his throat which set off deep coughing spasms, causing him to drop his glass. The shattering sound got her attention and Mychal turned around to see a flushed Richard trying to catch his breath. She walked over and said, "You are going to bed. Now. Back stairs, let's go."

He nodded and put his arm around her for support as they climbed the back stairs. Her touch electrified him. Once in their room, Richard collapsed in their bed. Mychal pulled off his jeans and shirt then retrieved his pajama bottoms from the bathroom. Once he was in bed, she pulled up the covers. She avoided looking directly at him, "Will you be all right?"

"Yes. Thank you." When she turned to leave again, he tried another delay tactic, "Mychal, please do not go. I mean, I know you hate me but I really need a little help. I was going to the kitchen to fix some lunch to take medication. I am afraid if I take it on an empty stomach I will get sick."

His words stung. "I never said I hated you. Listen, I'm going to get the glass up, bring you something to take the medication and then I have to leave. I can't stay."

Some minutes later she returned with a bowl of grapes with sliced cheese and crackers. Then she arranged his pillows and put his lunch tray at the foot of the bed. Richard sat on the edge of the bed and pushed the tray away, making a face.

"What's wrong now?" She was anxious to leave before she lost her composure.

"I'm not hungry. I never was, I just wanted you to stay. I need you here. Not only because I need to talk to you, but because I honestly need you. Please, just stay and talk." He moved quickly and imprisoned her hand.

"What do you want to talk about? I'm in legal trouble at home. I ended up pregnant right in the middle of that chaos. And worse yet, in less than a hundred and twenty days I will be unemployed. There, we talked."

"Just stop. Stop trying to argue. It will

not help anything, nor deter me." He let out a heartfelt sigh but continued to hold her hand. "Now, we need to start with the unsaid things between us. For example, your situation in the States. Explain it to me so I can understand."

Mychal moved toward the window with Richard still holding her hand. She eyed the door but remembered he just said he was not going to be deterred. It was time to face the music. "As I said, my brother-in-law was a financial consultant. With the profits from my book, he made money for me. Then he came up with this plan where we could get government grants for a business. He wanted a financial firm for non profit organizations and said I would be a financial backer. That is **not** what he did. He took that money, invested it on an insider tip and made an unbelievable fortune. He gave me back triple what I invested. He and my sister bought a big house up in Scarsdale, a boat, nice cars and so on. Me, I was careful because I knew something could go wrong. I bought a couple of cars, my houses and took care of my mother. My money is in bank accounts everywhere."

"The government finally caught up with Jake. They froze his accounts and seized him and Riley's assets. They have nothing and have moved into my mother's house. There is a good chance that he is going to prison and he is trying to take me with him. My things are protected and are not tied to any of his schemes. Most of my properties are legally protected, so they cannot be touched. Now they want me for questioning or whatever. But I think I'm moving to London where hopefully I will be left alone until this whole mess blows over. And that's the whole story."

"Why did you not tell me? I would have understood."

"I had planned to! A few times I tried to! But there was no rush until his dumb ass got arrested and started trying to take me down with him!" She wailed, unable to control her emotions anymore, "Then of all things, I found out I was pregnant. It looked like a trap to me, so I thought you would look at a pregnancy like that too. I knew you loved me, but what would this baby mean to you? After that night with Demitri, I knew you would resent my dishonesty and possibly my baby too, so I left."

"Come here Mychal." He moved the tray. She sat down on the bed and Richard held her hands. "I love you. I loved you before that night and I loved you before the baby. That night Demitri stood accusing you of such horrible things and you said nothing. You would not even look at me. I do not know which hurt worst; the fact you were not totally honest with me or the fact you were too ashamed to trust me. That did not change the way I felt about you. I gave you my word. These weeks have been miserable. I just love you and I want you in my life under any condition and regardless of the circumstance."

"I need to think. I need time and I need space. I just need to leave," she tried to pull away.

"No, I will not let you. Stop running. Stop leaving every situation in which you cannot control all the factors. I know you are not trying to trap me. I know you love me. Please stop feeling guilty. I wanted to marry you before the baby and I want to marry you now for the same reasons. Not because it is my duty, but because I want to spend the rest of my life with you. *¿Comprenda?*" The urgency of his tone tore at her heart.

"I can't Richard. Do you realize the gravity of my situation? Alone, pregnant. almost unemployed, and in serious legal trouble."

"You are not alone. I am asking you to marry me. What do you need, an official proposal?" He got down on one knee.

After a coughing spell, he said, "Mychal Scott Ayscue, will you please be my wife?"

"Richard, you sound like the grim reaper crawled into your lungs. Get up and back in bed." He did not move.

"There, you are not alone. Also, I bought us some time in your legal and local troubles. Two American officials from the embassy called me today. I was vague with them about the person the university hired for the position. As far as they know from me, you are not here. They called right after the authorities came to see me about you assaulting and attempting to kill Demitri."

"What the hell? I know I hit her hard but she was alive when I left. What happened? What did you do?" Mychal was suddenly worried she was going to have a new legal battle. She was also secretly wishing the other woman was dead or on death's doorstep.

"The same thing that happened the last time we broke up, she got the authorities involved with her deception," all Richard could do was shake his head. "But I hope I fixed that situation. After talking with the authorities, they have a background of her violent and deceptive behavior and witnesses to corroborate the truth of what really happened here at the house that night. They are wanting to talk with you for a statement but I told them you were away on a small holiday. I took their cards so you could contact them upon your return. I have already set it up that you were another victim of her bizarre behavior so please do not go rogue and say that you meant to kill her."

"Very clever man. Wait. What? She reported I tried to kill her?'

"And that you attacked her in a restaurant?"

Mychal looked at the scar in her palm, "Yeah, that was when I broke a glass and kicked a table into the chair while she was sort of sitting in it. She threatened me and I thought a table in the throat would set her straight. I earned the stitches for that one."

She held up her hand.

Richard knew this was not the time to scold, but said, "Oh I see what you did there. You told me just enough truth to keep me from questioning or worrying. Clumsy my ass. It never occurred to you to tell your friend, lover, possible husband, support system and father of your child that his ex-girlfriend who threatened him in the past threatened you?"

"I thought I handled it. I have always handled things alone and in my own way," she replied quietly.

"And now? What about now because we are together? We are as one. Mychal, is trying to give you a life with me so wrong? *Bella* without you, I am empty and every day has no meaning." He looked directly in

her eyes and straight into her soul,
"Without you all that I am will slowly die.
If you love me like you say you do, would
you let the same woman take you away
from me and do that to me again?"

The thought made her cringe as she
remembered their argument in the car.
Finally, she bent and kissed him. "Without
you, I too am lost. I love you and don't
want to live a life without you in it. As you
said, we are one."

Richard beamed into her face, "Is that a
yes then? *¿Mi esposa, mi corazón?*

"I don't' know exactly what you
said, but my answer is yes," she grinned.
Richard was up and pulling Mychal into a
crushing hug.

"Oh sorry. Sorry *nino* or *nina,,*"
Richard laughed then coughed, "Now *Bella*,
I will get some rest. But I want you beside
me. I want to hold you so I can feel our
baby."

Richard finally got into bed and Mychal kicked off her shoes to slide in bed beside him. Smiling she put both their hands on her hardening abdomen. Richard looked at her with an ear splitting grin.

"What are you grinning about? If it's what I think, we will have to check with the OBGYN first," she joked.

Richard laughed, "I had not thought of that, but do not temp me. I am just glad to have you back in my arms. It is hard to believe I am going to marry the woman that I thought was a man when she was hired. If you had not bullied poor Pedro into bringing you here, none of this would have happened. That and we are going to be parents. I love you."

"I love you Roman Ricardo García-Torres. I never meant to hurt you," Mychal looked into his dark green eyes. Her voice grew weak, "I was just so . . ."

Richard kissed the top of her head and

pulled her closer, "I know *Bella*, I know. All is forgiven. You really have to marvel though, how a simple mistake on a foreign exchange program application bought you into my life."

"That and the shady dealings of my weird family. Let's give credit where credit is due," Mychal huffed.

"Well Papa used to say when the time is right all things will line up and work together for the good." Richard looked at her with nostalgia and love.

She smiled at him, "Your parents were wise and shared a lifetime of love."

He smiled back, "They were and we will too."

¿Finalisado?

ABOUT THE AUTHOR

Sean Scott Kerns currently lives in the Hampton Roads area of Virginia. Sean's previous works have been published in the *Rhapsody in Black* magazine since the early 1990s. Sean's passions include travel and martial arts. The Foreign Exchange is Sean's first novel. Follow the next chapter in Mychal and Richard's story as it continues in the *Foreign Engagement*.

Check out her website at

www.seanscottkerns.com

www.ingramcontent.com/pod-product-compliance
Lightning Source LLC
Chambersburg PA
CBHW062140170626
46813CB00002B/757